"MORTARS!" SOMEONE YELLED.

"Double-time!" Falconi ordered.

The Black Eagle detachment surged forward at a rapid trot and broke through the tree line into a clearing. The North Vietnamese mortar crew looked at the sudden appearance of the Americans with a mixture of shock and fear. Nine M16 rifles emptied their magazines into the hapless mortarmen. The NVA died at their weapon, their bodies falling amidst the ammo boxes.

Archie looked at what was left of the mortar crew. "These guys won't bother us no more, sir."

"Yeah," Falconi agreed. "But we can't go back. There's nothing there but the rest of the North Vietnamese Army. The real problem comes tomorrow when we cross the Chinese border."

"Yeah," Archie said. "Then it's *really* going to hit the fan!"

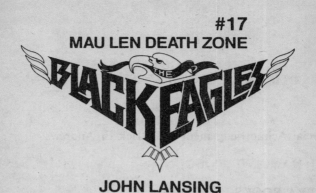

#17
MAU LEN DEATH ZONE
THE BLACK EAGLES

JOHN LANSING

ZEBRA BOOKS
KENSINGTON PUBLISHING CORP.

Special Acknowledgement to Patrick E. Andrews

ZEBRA BOOKS

are published by

Kensington Publishing Corp.
475 Park Avenue South
New York, NY 10016

First printing: November, 1988

Printed in the United States of America

*This book is dedicated to
the magnificent paratroopers of
the 456th Parachute Field Artillery Battalion
of World War II*

The Black Eagles Roll of Honor

(Assigned or Attached Personnel Killed in Action)

Sergeant Barker, Toby—U.S. Marine Corps
Sergeant Barthe, Eddie—U.S. Army
Sergeant Bernstein, Jacob—U.S. Marine Corps
First Lieutenant Blum, Marc—U.S. Air Force
Sergeant Boudreau, Marcel—U.S. Army
Chief Petty Officer Brewster, Leland—U.S. Navy
Specialist Four Burke, Tiny—U.S. Army
Sergeant Carter, Demond—U.S. Army
Master Sergeant Chun, Kim—South Korean Marines
Staff Sergeant Dayton, Marvin—U.S. Army
Sergeant Fotopoulus, Dean—U.S. Army
Sergeant First Class Galchaser, Jack—U.S. Army
Lieutenant Hawkins, Chris—U.S. Navy
Sergeant Hodges, Trent—U.S. Army
Mister Hosteins, Bruno—ex-French Foreign Legion
Petty Officer Second Class Jackson, Fred—U.S. Navy
Chief Petty Officer Jenkins, Claud—U.S. Navy
Petty Officer First Class Johnson, Sparks—U.S. Navy
Specialist Four Laird, Douglas—U.S. Army
Sergeant Limo, Raymond—U.S. Army
Petty Officer Third Class Littleton, Michael—U.S. Navy
Sergeant Makalue, Jessie—U.S. Army
Lieutenant Martin, Buzz—U.S. Navy

Petty Officer Second Class Martin, Durwood—U.S. Navy

Sergeant Matsamura, Frank—U.S. Army

Staff Sergeant Maywood, Dennis—U.S. Army

Sergeant First Class Miskoski, Jan—U.S. Army

Staff Sergeant Newcomb, Thomas—Australian Army

First Lieutenant Nguyen Van Dow—South Vietnamese Army

Staff Sergeant O'Quinn, Liam—U.S. Marine Corps

Sergeant First Class Ormond, Norman—U.S. Army

Staff Sergeant O'Rourke, Salty—U.S. Marine Corps

Sergeant Park, Chun Ri—South Korean Marines

Sergeant First Class Rivera, Manuel—U.S. Army

Petty Officer Third Class Robichaux, Richard—U.S. Navy

Sergeant Simpson, Dwayne—U.S. Army

Master Sergeant Snow, John—U.S. Army

Staff Sergeant Taylor, William—Australian Army

Lieutenant Thompson, William—U.S. Navy

Staff Sergeant Tripper, Charles—U.S. Army

Staff Sergeant Valverde, Enrique—U.S. Army

First Lieutenant Wakely, Richard—U.S. Army

Staff Sergeant Whitaker, George—Australian Army

Gunnery Sergeant White, Jackson—U.S. Marine Corps

Roster of the Black Eagles

Lieutenant Colonel Robert Falconi
U.S. Army
Commanding Officer
(17th Black Eagle Mission)

First Lieutenant Ray Swift Elk
U.S. Army
Executive Officer
(15th Black Eagle Mission)

Sergeant Major Top Gordon
U.S. Army
Operations Sergeant
(15th Black Eagle Mission)

Sergeant First Class Calvin Culpepper
U.S. Army
Demolitions Supervisor
(15th Black Eagle Mission)

Sergeant First Class Malcomb McCorckel
U.S. Army
Medical Corpsman
(15th Black Eagle Mission)

Staff Sergeant Paulo Garcia
U.S. Marine Corps
Intelligence/Communications
(7th Black Eagle Mission)

Sergeant Gunnar Olson
U.S. Army
Logistics
(5th Black Eagle Mission)

Petty Officer 3rd Class Blue Richards
U.S. Navy
Demolitions Specialist
(10th Black Eagle Mission)

Sergeant Archie Dobbs
U.S. Army
Detachment Scout
(15th Black Eagle Mission)

Prologue

The cell door opened and the prisoner was yanked roughly off the wooden bunk. The guard pushed him toward the cell door. *"Di thi di!"* he commanded.

The captive, electric shock burns over his body, was dressed in baggy, striped prison clothing that were too large for him. Barefoot and demoralized, he had once worn the bemedaled uniform befitting his position of colonel in the South Vietnamese army. But all his former dignity had been beaten and shouted away after months of confinement and torture.

He started to sob quietly as they went down the hall. He knew this would be another session of brutality as they continued to wring him dry of all the intelligence he had on clandestine operations in North Vietnam. He had already told them everything he knew, but the Reds continued to use abusive questioning in order to check and recheck his revelations.

But this time they did not stop at the dreaded interrogation chamber. They went on down to another door. This one opened into a rather plain, but pleasant office.

An NVA major pointed to a neatly folded stack of clothing. "Get dressed, Phuong!"

The prisoner, Colonel Phuong Bai, quickly obeyed. He was surprised at the quality of the attire. Although it was only a Chinese manufactured denim suit, it felt wonderfully clean and well fitting to him. After dressing, he was ushered by the major out another door and down a hallway. They passed through one more portal and stepped out into an alley where an automobile waited. Phuong barely had time to notice it was night before he received another curt instruction.

"Inside!"

The prisoner dully obeyed. After they had settled in, a young soldier-driver started up the car. They went through the dark streets until they were outside of the city traveling down a rural highway. A half hour later, the car was turned off onto a side road. They finally stopped after going a short distance to a place where another vehicle waited. A high-ranking officer stood by this other conveyance, calmly smoking a cigarette.

The major pointed out the window at the other officer. "Report to the comrade general!"

Phuong got out of the car and walked slowly up to the officer. He stopped and looked at the man illuminated by the headlights. The general came close, speaking in low tones. "Do not show surprise or any emotion, Colonel Phuong," he whispered.

Phuong was taken aback by the almost intimate politeness. Dull-eyed and weary, he simply waited to see what would happen next.

The North Vietnamese general's next words shocked the prisoner to full alertness. "I wish to defect from the north. The driver and officer over there know nothing about it."

Colonel Phuong, confused and frightened, licked his dry lips. "I don't know what I can do."

"I can get you back to your side through a clandestine E&E net of my own. You can arrange for someone to come and pick me up. Once I am in the south, you can escort me to the right people," the general

12

said. "That is all that I require of you. Do you not wish to rejoin your army and government? Do you not wish to see your wife and family again?"

"Yes," Phuong said sorrowfully. "But I have betrayed my country under questioning."

"I will tell them you did not break," the general said. "You will be a hero."

The prisoner's hopes rose. "But how do I know I can trust you?"

"Wait." The general left him, walking slowly over to the other car. When he arrived, he engaged the others in conversation, begging a cigarette and match. Suddenly he stepped back, pulling a Russian Tokarev automatic pistol from his holster. He fired twice quickly. Then he turned and beckoned to the prisoner. *Tien len!*

Phuong obediently went over to the general. He looked down at the bodies in the headlights. Both were truly dead, bits of brains sticking out from their head wounds.

"Now do you believe me?" the general asked.

"Co, Dai Tuong," Phuong said nodding.

"When you are back in South Vietnam, tell your intelligence people that I will be available at the coastal army rest center north of Ha Coi," the general said.

"Ha Coi? That is almost in China!" the prisoner exclaimed.

"It will be dangerous for those who come to fetch me, but I am worth such a risk," the general said.

"Yes. Of course," Phuong said. *"Xin loi ong,* but whom shall I say is defecting, General?"

The officer smiled. "They will know who I am when you tell them my name is Truong Van."

Chapter 1

Chuck Fagin walked from the shade of the big aircraft hangar, out into the blistering sunlight. He pulled a handkerchief from his pocket and mopped at the sweat streaming down his face. In spite of the dark sunglasses he wore, Fagin had to squint his eyes against the brilliance as he scanned the horizon for a glimpse of the aircraft he was waiting for.

A feminine voice called out to him from the hangar. "Can you see them yet?"

He shook his head and walked back inside to join Andrea Thuy. "Nope." He wiped his pudgy face again. "Damn! It's hard to believe that a couple of weeks ago we were in the middle of monsoon."

Andrea, who had spent part of the rainy weather as a captive of both the Viet Cong and the North Vietnamese Army, only smiled at him. "This is Southeast Asia, Chuck. You're either going to be sopping wet with rain or with perspiration."

"I'll take the rain. At least the temperature—" He stopped speaking. "Was that an aircraft I just heard?"

"Yes," Andrea said pointing outward. "Off in the distance."

A small speck above the horizon slowly approached them. As it grew larger, its shape gradually changed until wings and a tail section could be easily dis-

15

cerned. Within ten minutes the fully recognizable C-130 aircraft had turned onto its final approach pattern, coming in for a landing at Peterson Field in Saigon where Chuck Fagin and Andrea Thuy impatiently waited for its arrival.

It landed on a far runway, taxiing up toward them. Its four T56 turboprop engines, even when feathered back, roared loudly. The airplane rolled up to the hangar and turned before coming to a complete stop. A couple of minutes later the door in the fuselage opened and the steps were pushed down into position.

Fagin and Andrea watched as the first passenger disembarked. This was Lieutenant Colonel Robert Falconi, commanding officer of the Black Eagle Detachment. Tall, with a sinewy slimness, he strode toward them in long, easy steps. He wore his patrol harness with pack, canteens, and ammunition pouches while carrying his M16 rifle in his hand. A jungle rucksack was slung over one of the colonel's broad shoulders.

The next man off the C-130 was First Lieutenant Ray Swift Elk. This full-blooded Sioux Indian was lean and muscular. His copper-colored skin, hawkish nose, and high cheekbones gave him the appearance of the classic prairie warrior. The great artists of the American West, Remington and Russell, could have used him as the perfect model in their portrayals of the noble Red Man. But beneath this outward appearance, Ray Swift Elk had one hell of an army service record. As a matter of fact, there were still dark spots on his fatigues where he'd removed his master sergeant chevrons after his battlefield commission. Brand new cloth insignia of an infantry lieutenant were sewn on his collar.

Twelve years of service in Special Forces had made Swift Elk particularly well-qualified to be the detachment executive officer. This particular position was important because, in reality, he was Falconi's second-in-command.

In spite of his skills and education in modern soldiering, Swift Elk still considered his ancestral past an important part of his life, and he practiced Indian customs when and where able. Part of his tribe's history included some vicious combat against the Black troopers of the U.S. Cavalry's 9th and 10th Cavalry Regiments of the racially segregated army of the 19th century. The Sioux warriors had nicknamed the black men they fought "Buffalo Soldiers." This was because of their hair which, to the Indians, was like the thick manes on the buffalo. The appellation was a sincere compliment because these native Americans venerated the bison. Ray Swift Elk called Calvin Culpepper, the black guy in the detachment, "Buffalo Soldier," and he did so with the same respect his ancestors demonstrated toward Uncle Sam's black horse troopers during the violent plains wars.

The next man to step onto the runway was Sergeant Major Top Gordon. As the senior non-commissioned officer of the Black Eagles, he was tasked with several administrative and command responsibilities. Besides having to take any issued operations plans and use them to form the basic operations orders for the missions, he was also responsible for maintaining discipline and efficiency within the unit.

Top was a husky man, his jet-black hair thinning perceptibly, looking even more sparse because of the strict G.I. haircut he wore. His entrance into the Black Eagles had been less than satisfactory. After seventeen years spent in the army's elite spit-and-polish airborne infantry units, he had brought in an attitude that did not fit well with the diverse individuals in Falconi's command. Gordon's zeal to follow army

17

regulations to the letter had cost him a marriage when his wife, fed up with having a husband who thought more of the army than her, filed for divorce and took their kids back to the old hometown in upstate New York. Despite that heartbreaking experience, he hadn't let up a bit. To make the situation for him even more difficult during his first days in the Black Eagles, he had taken the place of a popular detachment sergeant who was killed in action on the Song Bo River. This noncom, called "Top" by the men, was an old Special Forces man who knew how to handle the type of soldier who volunteered for unconventional units. Any new top sergeant would have been resented no matter what type of man he was.

Gordon's premier appearance in his new assignment brought him into quick conflict with the Black Eagle personnel. Within only hours, the situation had gotten so far out of hand that Falconi began to seriously consider relieving the sergeant and seeing to his transfer back to a regular airborne unit.

But during Operation Laos Nightmare, Gordon's bravery under fire earned him the grudging respect of the lower-ranking Black Eagles. Finally, when he fully realized the problems he had created for himself, he changed his methods of leadership. Gordon backed off doing things by the book and found he could still maintain good discipline and efficiency while getting rid of the chicken-shit aspects of army life. It was most apparent he had been accepted by the men when they bestowed the nickname "Top" on him.

He had truly become the "top sergeant" then. But his natural gruffness and short temper remained the same. Nothing could change those characteristics.

The detachment medic, Sergeant First Class Malcomb "Malpractice" McCorckel, an original member of the unit, was always right on Top Gordon's

18

heels as he stepped off the aircraft. An inch under six feet in height, Malpractice had been in the army for twelve years. He had a friendly face and spoke softly as he pursued his duties in seeing after the illnesses and hurts of his buddies. He nagged and needled each and every one of them in order to keep that wild bunch healthy. They bitched back at him, but not angrily, because each Black Eagle appreciated the medical sergeant's concern. They all knew that nothing devised by puny man—not even mortar fire or grenades—could keep Malpractice from reaching a wounded detachment member and pulling him back to safety. Malpractice was unique in the unit for another reason too. He was the only married man under Falconi's command.

The detachment's slowest, easiest going guy, Petty Officer Blue Richards was next in the airplane's door. He was a fully-qualified Navy Seal. Besides his fighting skills, his special claim to fame was his uncanny tree-climbing abilities. When it was necessary to go high to get a good look around, Blue could be counted on to shimmy up even the tallest trees. A red-haired Alabamian with a gawky, good-natured grin common to good ol' country boys, Blue had been named after his "daddy's favorite huntin' dawg." An expert in demolitions either on land or underwater, Blue considered himself honored for his father to have given him that dog's name.

Right behind Blue came Marine Staff Sergeant Paulo Garcia. Under the new reorganization of the detachment that was necessary after suffering such heavy casualties, Paulo performed both the communications and intelligence work for the Black Eagles. Of Portuguese descent, this former tuna fisherman from San Diego, California, had joined the marines at the relatively late age of twenty-one after deciding to look

19

for a bit of adventure. There was always Marine Corps activity to see around his hometown, and he decided that fighting group offered him exactly what he was looking for. Ten years of service and plenty of combat action in the Demilitarized Zone and Khe Sanh made him more than qualified for the Black Eagles.

Sergeant First Class Calvin Culpepper was a tall, brawny black man who had entered the Army off a poor Georgia farm his family had worked as sharecroppers. Although once a team leader in the detachment, the new set-up got him back to his usual job of handling all the senior demolition chores. His favorite tool in that line of work was C4 plastic explosive. It was said he could set off a charge under a silver dollar and get back ninety-nine cents change. Resourceful, intelligent, and combatwise, Calvin, called the "Buffalo Soldier" by Lieutenant Ray Swift Elk, pulled his weight—and then a bit more—in the dangerous undertakings of the Black Eagles.

The newest man was Army Sergeant Gunnar Olson who had officially taken part in one Black Eagle mission before his actual assignment to the detachment. This had been during the operation on the Song Cai River when he'd been a gunner—appropriately called Gunnar the Gunner—on a helicopter gunship that flew fire support operations for Falconi and his men. Gunnar was so impressed with the detachment that he immediately put in for a transfer to the unit. Falconi quickly approved the paperwork and hired Gunnar the Gunner on as the unit's heavy weapons man. Now armed with an M70 grenade launcher and a .45 caliber automatic pistol, Gunnar, of Norwegian descent from Minnesota, looked forward to continued service with the detachment, despite the mauling they'd taken on their last mission.

The man with the most perilous job in the detachment was Archie Dobbs, and no other unit in the army had a man quite like him. Formerly a brawling, beer-swilling womanizer, Archie had been a one-man public scandal and disaster area in garrison or in town. But that was before he'd found his new love, Army nurse Betty Lou Pemberton. Now his wild ways had tamed down quite a bit. But, out of control or not, Archie was out in the field as point man and scout. In that job he went into the most dangerous areas first.

That was his trade: to see what—or who—was there. Reputed to be the best compass man in the United States Army, his seven years of service were fraught with stints in the stockade and dozens of "busts" to lower rank. Fond of women and booze, Archie's claim to fame—and the object of genuine respect from the other men—was that he had saved their asses on more than one occasion by guiding them safely through throngs of enemy troops behind the lines. Like the cat who always landed on his feet, Archie could be dropped into the middle of any geographic hell and find his way out. His sense of direction was flawless and had made him the man-of-the-hour on several Black Eagle missions during dangerous exfiltration operations when everything had gone completely and totally to hell.

A mini-reunion of sorts occurred inside the hangar. Chuck Fagin—the man the Black Eagles loved to hate—shook hands with the men and traded wisecracks. Andrea, who had not seen them in several weeks, had to endure some bear hugs and wet kisses on the cheek before she was finally allowed to embrace the one man she really loved—Robert Falconi.

"Okay, guys," Fagin announced. "I have a bus waiting for you on the other side of the building. It ain't air conditioned, but it's got wheels."

"Better'n walking," Sergeant Major Top Gordon

said agreeably. He turned to the others. "What the hell are you jokers waiting for? Move it!"

They crowded aboard the olive-drab G.I. bus and settled in for the short ride. When all were aboard, Fagin tapped the driver's shoulder. The vehicle pulled away from the hangar and took a direct route across the small airbase until it arrived at a compound surrounded by barbed wire.

An ARVN guard unit, complete with heavy .50 caliber machine guns, was stationed around the area. The commanding officer, a short but tough-looking captain, would only permit the Black Eagles off the bus one at a time as he personally checked their I.D. cards against a roster he'd been given.

Finally, after more than twenty minutes of scrutiny, the final man, Archie Dobbs, walked through the wire and went into the building to join the others.

This was an area officially designated as "Isolation." The name for the place was absolutely correct. The Black Eagle Detachment was cut off from the outside world. No one was allowed in or out without special clearance and permission. Such activities were part of the Special Operations Group's standing operating procedures. The arrangement, though confining and aggravating to the personnel concerned, guaranteed the strictest observance of security and secrecy. Although no one said anything, they all knew they were inside the Isolation Area for only one reason—there was a mission in the offing.

The men were left to themselves while Lieutenant Colonel Robert Falconi and First Lieutenant Ray Swift Elk withdrew to a side room with Chuck Fagin and Andrea Thuy. A couple of card games began along with a general bullshit session as the guys turned their attention to a little enjoyment.

The one exception was Archie Dobbs.

Normally he was the most boisterous of the Black Eagles, but his recent break-up with his sweetheart had toned down his emotions a great deal. The object of his affections, Lieutenant Betty Pemberton of the Army Nurse Corps, had completed her tour in Vietnam. She had given Archie an ultimatum: Either give up the Black Eagles or her. He'd chosen to remain in the detachment. When Betty Lou received her orders to return to the States, she'd not even bothered to say goodby to him.

"Hey, Archie!" Calvin Culpepper called from a poker game. "C'mon and play, man. I need your money."

Archie only smiled weakly. "No thanks. I guess I ain't in the mood."

The guys all knew his problem and sympathized with him. Blue Richards, sensitive and sapient despite his rural upbringing, waved his cards at Archie. "I'm just about broke here, ol' buddy. Suppose I git outta this here game and you and me have a coupla beers outta that cooler. We could jaw awhile. Whattaya say, Archie?"

Archie nodded gratefully. "That'd be fine, Blue."

But before they could get to their B.S. session, their two officers emerged from the room with Chuck Fagin and Andrea Thuy. Andrea waved to the guys. "Be seeing you later."

"Yeah," Fagin said following her to the door. "Write if you get work."

Falconi waited until they left, then he turned to the men. He held up a bundle of papers in his hands. "Know what these are?"

There was a groan from the detachment. Archie, who didn't give a damn one way or the other, walked over and looked at the documents. "OPLANs," he said.

23

Ray Swift Elk nodded his head. "And we all know what that means, don't we?"

No one said a word. The quick transfer from Camp Nui Dep back to Peterson Field's Isolation Area had been indication enough:

An operation was going down.

Chapter 2

The acronym OPLAN, used by Archie Dobbs to refer to the papers in the bundle that Falconi held in his hands, stood for Operations Plan.

An OPLAN is a brief concept of how a scheduled operation or mission should be conducted. The particular one that Fagin carried into the billets at Peterson Field had been aptly designated as *OPLAN Operation Mau Len Rescue*. This document was written by the staff at Special Operations Group on the other side of that same Peterson Field. That particular team of officers wanted a specific job carried out. Even at that high level of echelon, it was not considered to be "etched in stone." Instead, it was actually a set of guidelines and information supplied to Lieutenant Colonel Robert Falconi and his men so that they could assimilate the information supplied and add their own input along with other data to create another, much more authoritative paper that would be called the OPORD (Operation Order).

The OPORD was written along strick guidelines that divided it into five basic paragraphs as follows:

1. SITUATION

a. Enemy Forces: (This was the strength, activity, identification, etc. of the bad guys that Falconi and his men were going to face.)

b. Friendly Forces: (These were the good joes that would be participating—or at least be located damned close—to them during Operation Mau Len Rescue. This included special notes on support capabilities, coordination, cooperation, etc. In most Black Eagle missions this paragraph was labeled "N/A"—Not Applicable—since the detachment would be out in the boonies operating on their own.)

2. MISSION

(A simple statement saying exactly what the Black Eagles were supposed to accomplish.)

3. EXECUTION

a. Concept of the Operation: (The "How-It's-Gonna-Be-Done" paragraph which included times, dates, organization, specific duties, etc.)

4. ADMINISTRATION AND LOGISTICS

    a. Rations

    b. Arms and Ammunition

    c. Uniforms and Equipment

    d. Special (Handling of wounded, prisoners, etc.)

5. COMMAND AND SIGNAL

    a. Signal: (Equipment, call signs, etc.)

    b. Command: (The chain of command.)

Lieutenant Colonel Robert Falconi broke open the bundle and quickly passed out the documents to the detachment. Each Black Eagle took his personal copy of the OPLAN and retired to begin his work on the portion of the mission that required his specialization. This was the brain work behind any operation, and it required concentration and meticulous attention to detail.

There were nine small field desks situated in the isolation billets. Every man had his own individual area in which to tend to his task. The work stations boasted portable G.I. typewriters, reams of paper, and two-drawer army file cabinets constructed of stiff cardboard. These were the "offices" where the men would write the annexes to the OPLAN to be submitted to Falconi for approval.

First Lieutenant Ray Swift Elk, as the executive officer, planned the overall operational concept. He worked hand-in-hand with Sergeant Major Top Gordon who would plan out the various execution phases of the mission.

Malpractice McCorckel was busy with medical items such as evacuation of casualties, sanitary conditions, data on disease and other health conditions in the operational area, and the prevention of sickness and injury wherever possible. He would coordinate his need for special supplies with Gunnar Olson who handled all logistical needs of the detachment. Any ammunition, weaponry, special equipment, or other S4 functions were Gunnar's responsibility.

Marine Staff Sergeant Paulo Garcia's job was to find out all he could about the enemy and even friendly troops that might be involved in the mission. Paulo made sure all the guys would be briefed in the latest information. He worked with Calvin Culpepper who had been given a special job of handling communications. Since that also involved allied units as well as the possibility of enemy interference or monitoring, the two Black Eagles had to be certain that all security and information channels were thoroughly covered.

Archie Dobbs and Blue Richards were assigned as "go-fers." They would fill in when needed and tend to any extra work that might pop up. Within moments of being issued the OPLANs, the entire Black Eagles Detachment settled into a routine of heavy, concentrated work.

All extra bullshitting and horseplay came to a halt.

The only sounds were those of clacking typewriters and the muted voices of men conferring with each other as the annexes to the OPLAN slowly took form.

Even after midnight, the work had not let up. Tired, sleepy men drinking black coffee continued their tasks, sewing up loose ends and filling in holes in this administrative preparation for combat violence.

Brigadier General James Taggart looked across his desk at Chuck Fagin. "Have there been any new evaluations on the risk factor of the Black Eagle mission?"

Fagin slowly shook his head. "Not at this time."

"Damn!"

Normally Fagin and Taggart were at odds with each other. But at that particular moment, both were in agreement on the special dangers and gamble involved—and the two men were very worried.

The intercom on the general's desk buzzed. He flipped the button on the device. "Yeah?"

"Colonel Phuong is here, General," the voice transmission reported.

"Send him in," Taggart ordered.

The door to the office opened and a sharply dressed South Vietnamese colonel wearing a chest full of ribbons stepped in. He saluted. "Colonel Phuong reporting as ordered, sir," he said in perfect English.

"How do you do, Colonel Phuong," Taggart said. "May I introduce Mister Fagin of the CIA?"

Fagin stood up to shake hands. But that was as much cordiality as he intended to display. "I have laid out a dozen photographic portraits on the general's desk, Colonel. Tell me if one of them is the man who identified himself to you as General Truong Van."

"I would be happy to, Mister Fagin."

28

Taggart stood up. "May I get you a drink, Colonel?"

"A scotch-and-soda would be fine." Phuong went over and examined the pictures. He picked one. "This is General Truong Van." He handed the photo to Fagin.

"Thank you," Fagin said.

"And this one," Phuong said getting another. "Also the far photograph, though it seems to have been taken years ago."

Fagin displayed an almost impish grin. "I just wanted to make sure you had not been a victim of a communist ploy to lure our Black Eagles up north."

"I understand, of course," Phuong said.

"Sit down, Colonel Phuong," the general invited as he handed the South Vietnamese officer a drink.

The colonel took a plush leather chair opposite Fagin. "Thank you."

"Tell me, Colonel," Fagin said. "Why do you think the general chose you to act as mediator in his defection to us?"

"I was under interrogation for quite a length of time," Phuong said. "They applied both psychological and physical torture on me during the rather lengthy periods of examination."

"Yes," Fagin said. "I have read the reports on your physical examination after you appeared in the south."

Phuong took a deep breath. "I—I did not break. Perhaps my actions convinced the general I also had the fortitude to make my way to safety if given the opportunity."

"What actions did the general take to convince you of his sincerity?" Fagin inquired.

"He killed his driver and an NVA officer in my presence," Phuong said.

"Then he simply gave you your freedom?"

29

Phuong laughed. "And a suit of Chinese clothing."

"Most generous," Fagin said.

"I beg your pardon, Mister Fagin," Phuong said. "But I have been through this previously. Is this line of questioning necessary or—" He paused and smiled again. "—valid?"

"I am emotionally involved," Fagin said.

"I don't quite understand," Phuong said.

"It means," Fagin said coldly, "that if the Black Eagles are compromised or betrayed, I might just kill somebody." He walked to the wet bar in the corner of the office and mixed himself a drink. "By the way, Colonel Phuong, congratulations on your award of the Cross of Gallantry."

"A token from my country," Phuong said. "For my conduct during captivity."

Fagin turned and raised his glass. "Here's to medals. And the poor sons of bitches that win 'em."

Phuong raised his own glass. "I'll drink to that, Mister Fagin."

Six folding chairs were arranged in a semi-circle facing an operational map mounted on the wall in front of the furniture. Calvin Culpepper, Malpractice Mc-Corckel, Paulo Garcia, Gunnar Olson, Blue Richards, and Archie Dobbs each sat in one. They held their copies of the annexes they had prepared on their laps as they waited for the briefing to begin.

After a straight thirty-six hours of work, Lieutenant Colonel Robert Falconi had finally blessed all the paperwork turning the OPLAN into an official OPORD—Operations Order.

The Black Eagles chatted in low voices among themselves. Although bone-weary, there was enough pre-mission adrenaline flowing through their bodies to give them extra energy. Only the heartbroken Archie Dobbs on the far end was silent. He stared down at the floor, his mood and morale at a low ebb.

"Tinch-*hut!*"

Top Gordon's loud voice broke across the room's quietness like the roar of an 81-millimeter mortar shell's detonation. The men snapped to attention. Falconi and Swift Elk came into the room.

"At ease," Falconi said. "Sit down, guys." He gave them a proud grin. "Looks like we're up to our necks again, huh? Well, the only thing I want to say at this time is for you to concentrate on your timing and details. We're going to be smack dab in the middle of the North Vietnamese Army, so let's be precise, decisive, and mean. That's it in a nutshell from me. I'll turn you over to Lieutenant Swift Elk and he'll give you the concept of the operation."

Ray went to the front of the room. "The mission is to go ashore in the vicinity of the NVA Rest Center at Ha Coi via submarine infiltration. Once there we'll make contact with a North Vietnamese general who wishes to defect. When contact is made with him, we'll pull back to the coast and meet the sub for exfiltration. That's it, cut and dried, but there's a few details to fill the in-betweens. I'll let Sergeant Major Gordon begin the ceremonies."

Top pulled out his annex. "We'll fall out tomorrow morning at 0400 ready to go. I say again—*ready to go!* That means you don't sack out tonight until I've checked you out completely and I personally know that you're prepared for the mission."

Paulo Garcia raised his hand. "That sounds like we're gonna have to sleep in our clothes, Sergeant Major."

"I don't care what you wear during beddy-bye," Top said. "But in the morning all you're going to have

31

out is what you're going to put on for the day's activities. You won't even comb your hair or brush your teeth. Now—we'll go by truck back to the airfield and board a C-130 for a plane trip to Nha Trang. Station time is 0445 and take-off is at 0500. That means we should arrive there NLT 0530. From there we'll go by launch out to our submarine."

Blue, a navy man, was curious. "Which sub is it, Sergeant Major?"

"The *Perch*," Top answered. "We'll get underway— as you swab jockeys say—immediately and should be in position to go ashore in our little rubber raft on 0200 the next morning."

"And what time do we pick up our wandering NVA general?" Malpractice McCorckel asked.

"About twenty-four hours later, then we'll head back for the coast to meet the *Perch*," Top said. "Once we're all on board the sub, we'll return to Nha Trang and our job is over. While the defector is being wined and dined, we'll be on our way back to good ol' Camp Nui Dep."

"Uff da!" Gunnar said in Norwegian. "Aren't we gonna get any time off here in Saigon?"

Top grinned. "In a word—no." He motioned to Paulo. "Let's have the intelligence portion of the briefing."

Paulo walked up to the front of the room and pointed to a place on the map that indicated a spot in North Vietnam near the Chinese border. "This," he announced, "is the location of the NVA's troop rest center at Ha Coi."

"Is that were we pick up our defector?" Calvin asked.

"It sure is," Paulo said.

"No sweat," Blue Richards said. "All them NVA guys will be relaxing when we come tippy-toeing in."

"Sorry," Paulo said shaking his head. "The North Vietnamese Army's concept of a rest and recreation area is not the same as ours. It simply means that the soldiers stationed there are away from active combat. They conduct field training exercises to keep toned up for their return to the fighting in the south."

"So what you're saying," Archie Dobbs interjected, "is that we'll have to move into a heavy concentration of battle-ready veteran enemy units, make contact with the defector, then return to the coast to meet our submarine without getting caught."

"That's exactly right," Paulo said. "We'll meet this general here—" He indicated a point on the map. "—five kilometers south of the center. The recognition challenge and password are 'Hot' and 'Potato.' When we're satisfied he is General Truong Van, we'll take him back with us."

"And if we're not sure?" Blue asked.

"We kill the guy and haul ass," Paulo said. He paused. "But if it ain't him, guys, then we've been set up. That leaves us only one contingency—fight our way back to the coast and hope we can link up with the sub."

"Who is this General Truong anyhow?" Malpractice McCorckel wanted to know.

"He's a high mucky-muck in NVA intelligence," Paulo explained. "He's worked closely with the Russian KGB in southeast Asia. Naturally the G2 boys are anxious to hear him spill his guts."

Falconi spoke from the back of the room. "It's a risky mission, guys. But worth it."

"If there are no more questions on intelligence, I'll let Calvin fill you in on commo," Paulo said.

Calvin "Buffalo Soldier" Culpepper stood up at his chair without going to the front of his audience. "It's real simple, dudes. We'll have four Prick-Six radios for commo between ourselves. The submarine will be able to communicate with us through them little radios too."

"Wait a minute!" Gunnar Olson protested. "They have limited range. We won't be able to talk to the sub unless we're damned good and close."

"Gunnar, my man," Calvin said with a sardonic grin. "If we ain't close to 'em, there ain't no sense in trying to have commo. That submarine ain't hanging around waiting for us. If we're late, we're forgotten. Understand?"

"Okay," Gunnar said. "So what about call signs?"

"Colonel Falconi is 'Falcon'," Calvin responded. "The other three radios are gonna belong to Lieutenant Swift Elk, the Sergeant Major, and Archie. The lieutenant is 'Elk' and the sergeant major is 'Top.' I thought I'd let Archie be 'Arch.' The submarine is 'Moby Dick.' "

"Mouldy Dick?" Archie asked.

"_Moby_ Dick, you dumb shit," Calvin said suppressing a laugh. "Like the whale in the book."

"Knock it off!" Top Gordon said. He pointed to Gunnar. "Any logistics to report?"

"Not much," Gunnar Olson replied. "We'll go in with a regular combat load on patrol harnesses. Since we're not supposed to be out in the cold too long there'll be no rucksacks or extra gear. And, naturally, no demo stuff. We'll tote M16s and .45s. The navy will give us the rubber boat. That's all we need."

"Thanks, Gunnar," Top said. Next he motioned to Malpractice. "Any medical poop?"

"Nothing to mention," Malpractice said. "I'll have my aid kit but no stretchers. Any non-walking wounded will have to be toted out on litters we make ourselves. The water in your canteens will be from the submarine so we shouldn't have to worry about getting any out of dirty creeks and rivers."

"Okay," Top said. "That's it. You're briefed. The operation is simple and straightforward. To sum it up: we go on a sub up to North Vietnam, go ashore and get a defecting NVA general, take him back to the sub, and return to South Vietnam." He paused. "Now listen up! There's cold beer in the cooler. I don't want anybody drinking any more after 2200 hours tonight. I'll hold a readiness inspection in one hour. After everyone—I say again—every swinging dick has shown me he's ready to shit and git, you can enjoy the brew. Any questions?"

"No, Sergeant Major!" they shouted.

"Then let's get back to work," Top said.

The Black Eagles were back in the war.

Chapter 3

A pale red glow bathed the interior of the submarine. The sub, the *U.S.S. Perch*, a *Balao* class boat, had been launched in September of 1943. Displacing 1,526 tons surfaced and 2,424 tons submerged, she was powered by a 2-shaft diesel 5400 horsepower engine that would push her through the waves at 20.25 knots. Under water, a two-shaft electric 2,740 horsepower engine would propel the sub at a top speed of 8.75 knots.

The *Perch* had seen plenty of action against the Japanese in the Pacific campaigns of World War II, but afterward she was converted as a troop carrier. The torpedo tubes and other non-essential equipment and instruments were stripped out and accommodations for passengers were installed. Both Blue Richards and Paulo Garcia had been aboard her before during training operations out of the Coronado Naval Station and Camp Pendleton in southern California.

The only troops aboard her now were the Black Eagle detachment. Most of the men, used to plenty of spacious outdoor living, felt cramped and a bit claustrophobic in the tubular confines of the submarine. Gunnar Olson lay in his bunk feeling the slight rolling of the boat as she moved through the underwater world. He turned his head and saw a sailor sitting in what appeared to be a closet. The man had a small portable typewriter on his knees on which he was typing some official form.

Curious, Gunnar slipped out of the rack and walked across the deck to the sailor. "Hi ya," the Black Eagle said.

"Hi," the sailor said with a quick glimpse up at him.

"Doing paperwork, huh?" Gunnar asked.

"Yeah," the submariner said. "I'm the boat's yeoman. That's like a clerk in the army."

"I see," Gunnar said. "How come you're typing in this here little closet? Why don't you go to your office?"

"Hell!" the sailor exclaimed. "This *is* my office."

"*Uff da,*" Gunnar said. "This submarine world is too small for me."

Another sailor appeared in the doorway. He had a tray full of sandwiches and cups of coffee. "Any o' you guys hungry?" he asked the Black Eagles.

The answer was a rush to the man as the seven enlisted men helped themselves to the food. The detachment's officers, Falconi, and Swift Elk, were up with the sub's captain going over last minute details.

"Hey, grilled cheese!" Calvin Culpepper exclaimed. "And nice and hot."

The yeoman had also availed himself of the chow. "It's one of the advantages of being on a pig boat," he exclaimed. "The galley is open twenty-four hours, even if it's only for coffee and doughnuts."

Gunnar turned to Archie Dobbs and whispered, "It ain't worth it! How'd you like to die in one o' these subs?"

Archie nodded. "A lot o' poor bastards have."

Colonel Phuong Bai made his way through the

crowd in the lobby of the Hotel Caravelle. He kept his eyes down to avoid making contact with any friends or acquaintances. The colonel turned into the cocktail lounge, finding a secluded spot at the end of the bar.

The bartender, an arrogant Vietnamese who hated his country's educated upperclass, tried to embarrass the officer by waiting on him in English. "Yes, sir? May I get you something?"

Phuong almost sneered. "Why certainly, my good man," he answered in the same language. "I would like a Dewars and soda with a twist. Hold the ice and make it a bit stiff, if you please."

The bartender smiled weakly. *"Co, Dai Ta."*

Phuong waited impatiently for his drink. When he got it, the ARVN officer drank it quickly in nervous gulps. He shoved the glass forward. "Another."

The bartender quickly complied.

Now Phuong sipped slowly, trying to stay as far back in the corner of the bar as possible. He saw a couple of his friends but was able to avoid eye contact with them. When that drink was finished, he ordered a third.

The crowd at the bar changed constantly. Most of the drinkers had other business at the hotel or were just meeting somebody there. Most had but one libation before leaving. Phuong's own presence there had been the result of a desire for a quick drink. But one had let to another until, after an hour, he was now nursing his fifth. His mood was so down that he could not muster the stamina to leave. It seemed much easier to continue to order more scotch and sodas.

"Colonel Phuong!"

He looked up at the sound of his name and saw an old army acquaintance. It was a major named Quyen with whom he had served on a battalion staff several years previously. Phuong, unable to get away, displayed a polite smile. "Good evening, Major Quyen."

Quyen came over and offered his hand. "I have only recently heard of your magnificent escape from captivity in the north."

"Yes," Phuong said. "I was very lucky."

"Do not be modest, Colonel," Quyen said. "Your name was in the official army newspaper. You were awarded the Cross of Gallantry. But they had no details other than saying you conducted yourself in a courageous and exemplary manner in spite of torture and threats to your life."

"One does one's duty," Phuong said. "There is no more to be said about it."

"I wouldn't care for any espionage and sabotage assignments in the north," Quyen said. "It was very brave of you to volunteer for such a dangerous mission."

"It was what I'd been trained for," Phuong said. "In the past I have dispatched many agents up there. It was only right that I took my turn."

"We are all very proud of you," Quyen said. "The Americans treat us like little brothers so much that it is good when one of our own kind demonstrates such magnificent soldierliness.

"You are too kind," Phuong said.

Quyen checked his watch. "I must go, Colonel. It was a great pleasure to see you. Allow me to congratulate you again on the medal for your valor."

"Thank you," Phuong said. He watched the other officer leave and finished off his drink. The colonel walked through the crowded bar and hurried across the lobby. Once outside he allowed the doorman to get him a cab.

The driver, disappointed he had not gotten a big-tipping American, spoke gruffly. *"Dau?"*

Phuong started to give him his home address but

39

suddenly changed his mind. "Take me to district Military Headquarters."

Wordlessly the cabbie slipped the automobile into gear and rolled into the slow traffic of Saigon. He leaned on his horn, blaring away with the other drivers as he threaded his way through the choked streets. Although the place was only eight blocks away it took almost twenty minutes to get there. Phuong, giving only a small tip, slipped out of the vehicle and stepped onto the curb. He walked across the sidewalk returning the salutes of the guards at the main entrance. He had to stop long enough to display his identification to a sergeant before going to the stairway to ascend the steps up to the second floor where his office was located.

The small room he'd been alloted held a chair, desk, and a floor lamp. His assignment upon returning to active duty had consisted of very light intelligence work. Phuong sat down at the desk without turning on the light. Somehow the dark was comforting to him. He sat there for a long, long time. Finally he reached over and switched on the lamp.

Phuong opened the desk drawer and pulled out the small box. Opening it, he looked dispassionately at the medal there. It was the South Vietnamese Army's Cross of Gallantry awarded him for his conduct while in the hands of the North Vietnamese.

It was all a big lie.

He'e broken quickly under torture. The Americans had a most apt term for what he'd done—Phuong had spilled his guts. Through his abject cowardice, he had compromised an entire net of operatives in the Hanoi area alone. All had been policed up and eventually shot. Now, to make matters even worse, there was a damned good chance that he had played an instrumental role in the destruction of colonel Robert

40

Falconi and his Black Eagle Detachment too.

Phuong replaced the medal. He reached farther back and pulled the .45 pistol in the drawer. The colonel was amazed at his own calmness as he slid the slide back and let it snap forward to chamber the chunky round from the top of the magazine. Then, swiftly and without hesitation, he slipped the muzzle into his mouth and pulled the trigger.

His brains and bits of skull splattered the wall behind him.

The submarine sailor standing at the bottom of the ladder nodded to Gunnar Olson. "Good luck."

"Yeah, thanks," Gunnar said. "I hope they let you move into a bigger office someday."

"No such luck, buddy," the yeoman said. "The cap'n's cabin ain't much bigger than what I got."

Gunnar grinned as he shoved his patrol harness upward to the hatch for Blue Richards to grab. The opening that led to the deck was so small that even that sparse bit of equipment could not be worn when going through it. The Black Eagle quickly ascended the rungs and squeezed thought the hatch. He stepped out on the deck and joined the rest of the detachment.

Everyone was busy under Sergeant Major Top Gordon's supervision. The men lashed down their equipment in the rubber boat they were to use for the infiltration phase of Operation Mau Len Rescue. Lieutenant Colonel Robert Falconi walked slowly around the activity, making sure everything was properly secured. Any mishap in the surf that caused the loss of weapons and equipment would be disastrous.

Falconi lifted his eyes long enough to gaze westward. The coast of enemy North Vietnam was just over the horizon. He looked northward. There was

Red China, gigantic and menacing, like a gargantuan anthill covered with billions of dutiful little zealots. If things went to shit on this mission, there would be no contingency plans regarding the north.

Falconi also thought about what awaited them on that North Vietnamese shore. A defecting general as prescribed? Or a trap that would finally sound the Black Eagles' swan song.

"Colonel Falconi?"

Falconi turned and saw the sub's skipper walking across the deck toward him. The naval officer held out his hand. "I guess you know the wish for good luck is sincere."

"And it's well appreciated," Falconi replied with a smile.

"I thought we'd review the pick-up phase quickly," the skipper said. We'll be back at this exact spot in twenty-four hours. We can give you a two-hour leeway unless North Vietnamese patrol boats show up. In that case, we'll submerge and haul ass."

"Right," Falconi said. "Then we can expect you back in another twenty-four hours."

"Yeah. For the second and final time." The submarine captain hesitated. "I'm afraid that if we don't make it then, that's the end of it. I'll be gone for good."

"Understood," Falconi said. "So long." He turned and went over to the boat, getting in at the coxswain's position. "Are you guys ready?"

"Sure," Archie Dobbs said. "Do you think we want to live forever?"

"Excuse me," Paulo Garcia interjected. "But I'd like it to go on the record that I, for one, would indeed like to live forever."

"Knock off the bullshit!" Top growled.

The submarine's crew were all now back inside. The

boat quivered a bit, then slowly submerged leaving the boat full of Black Eagles floating on the surface of the Gulf of Tonkin.

"Ready," Falconi softly called out. "Stroke! Stroke! Stroke! Port around starboard! Stroke! Give way together! Stroke! Stroke!"

With their paddles silently slipping into the water with each pull, the Black Eagles edged closer to the fate that awaited them on the enemy coast.

Holding his coxswain's paddle, their commander Robert Falconi felt nothing but pride and manly affection for those great guys. They asked nothing and gave all in following their motto of *Calcitra clunis*.

Lieutenant Colonel Robert Falconi felt he was the luckiest guy in the world to be their commanding officer.

Chapter 4

Robert Mikhailovich Falconi was born an Army brat at Fort Meade, Maryland in the year 1934.

His father, Second Lieutenant Michael Falconi was the son of Italian immigrants. The parents, Salvatore and Luciana Falconi, had wasted no time in instilling appreciation of America and the opportunities offered by the nation into the youngest son. They had already instilled deep patriotism into their seven other children. Mister Falconi even went as far as naming his son Michael rather than the Italian Michele. The boy had been born an American, was going to live as an American so—*per Dio e tutti i santi*—he was going to be named as an American!

Young Michael was certainly no disappointment to his parents or older brothers and sisters. He studied hard in school and excelled. He worked in the family's small shoe repair shop in New York City's Little Italy during the evenings, doing his homework late at night. When he graduated from high school, Michael was eligible for several scholarships to continue his education in college, but even with this help, it would have entailed great sacrifice on the part of his parents. Two older brothers, beginning promising careers as lawyers, could have helped out a bit, but Michael didn't want to be any more of a burden on his family than was absolutely necessary.

He knew of an alternative. The nation's service academies, West Point and Annapolis, offered free education to qualified young men. Michael, through the local ward boss, received a congressional appointment to take the examinations to attend the United States Military Academy.

He was successful in this endeavor and was appointed to the Corps of Cadets. West Point didn't give a damn about his humble origins. It didn't matter to the Academy whether his parents were poor immigrants or not. West Point also considered Cadet Michael Falconi as socially acceptable as anyone in the Corps regardless of the fact that his father was a struggling cobbler. The only thing that concerned the institution was whether he, as an individual, could cut it or not. It was this measuring of a man by no other standards than his own abilities and talents that caused the young plebe to develop a sincere, lifelong love for the United States Army. He finished his career at the school in the upper third of his class, sporting the three chevrons and rockers of a brigade adjutant upon graduation.

Second Lieutenant Falconi was assigned to the Third Infantry Regiment at Fort Meade, Maryland. This unit was a ceremonial outfit that provided details for military funerals at Arlington National Cemetery, the guard for the Tomb of the Unknown Solider and other official functions in the Washington, D.C. area.

The young shavetail enjoyed the bachelor's life in the nation's capital, and his duties as protocol officer, though not too demanding, were interesting. He was required to be present during social occasions that were official ceremonies of state. He coordinated the affairs and saw to it that all the political bigwigs and other brass attending them had a good time. He was doing exactly those duties at such a function when he met a young Russian Jewish refugee named Miriam Ananova Silberman.

She was a pretty, twenty-year old brunette, who had the most striking eyes that Michael Falconi had ever seen. He would always say throughout his life that it was her eyes that captured his heart. When he met her, Miriam was a member of the League of Jewish Refugees, attending a congressional dinner. She and her father, Rabbi Josef Silberman, had recently fled the Red dictator Stalin's anti-Semitic terrorism in the Soviet Union. Her organization had been lobbying the American Congress to enact legislation that would permit the U.S. government to take action in saving European and Asian Jewry not only from the savagery of the communists but also from the Nazis in Germany who had only just begun their own program of intimidation and harassment of their country's Jewish population.

When the lieutenant met the refugee beauty at the start of the evening's activities, he fell hopelessly in love. He spent that entire evening as close to her as he could possibly be, while ignoring his other duties. A couple of congressmen who arrived late had to scurry around looking for their tables without aid. Lieutenant Falconi's full attention was on Miriam. He was absolutely determined he would get better acquainted with this beautiful Russian. He begged her to dance with him at every opportunity, was solicitous about seeing to her refreshments and engaged her in conversation, doing his best to be witty and interesting.

He was successful.

Miriam Silberman was fascinated by this tall, dark, and most handsome young officer. She was so swept off her feet that she failed to play the usual coquettish little games employed by most women. His infectious smile and happy charm completely captivated the young belle.

The next day Michael began a serious courtship, determined to win her heart and marry the girl.

Josep Silberman, her father, was a cantankerous, elderly widower. He opposed the match from the beginning. As a Talmud scholar he wanted his only daughter to marry a nice Jewish boy. But Miriam took pains to point out to him that this was America—a country that existed in direct opposition to homogeneous customs. The mixing of nationalities and religions was not that unusual in this part of the world. The rabbi argued, stormed, forbade and demanded—but all for naught. In the end, so he would not lose the affection of his daughter, he gave his blessing. The couple was married in a non-religious ceremony at the Fort Meade post chapel.

A year later their only child, a son, was born. He was named Robert Mikhailovich.

The boy spent his youth on various army posts. There were only two times he lived in a town or civilian neighborhood. The first was during the years his father, by then a colonel, served overseas in the European Theater of Operations in the First Infantry Division—the Big Red One. A family joke developed out of the colonel's service in that particular outfit. Robert would ask his dad, "Why are you serving in the First Division?"

The colonel always answered, "Because I figured if I was going to be One, I might as well be a Big Red One."

It was one of those private family jokes that don't go over too well outside the home.

The second stint of civilian living was in San Diego, California during the time that the colonel was assigned as the supervisor of that city's public school Reserve Officer Training Program

47

But despite this overabundance of martial neighborhoods, the boy had a happy childhood. The only problem was his dislike of school. Too many genes of ancient Hebrew warriors and Roman legionnaires danced through the youth's fiery soul. Robert was a kid who liked action, adventure and plenty of it. The only serious studying he ever did was in the karate classes he took when the family was stationed in Japan. He was accepted in one of that island nation's most prestigious martial arts academies where he excelled while evolving in a serious and skillful *karateka*.

His use of this fighting technique caused one of the ironies in his life. In the early 1950s, during the time his father headed up San Diego, California's high school ROTC program, Robert was himself a student—a most indifferent scholar at best. Always looking for excitement, his natural boldness got him into a run-in with some young Mexican-Americans. One of the Chicanos had never seen such devastation as that which Bobby Falconi dealt out with his hands. But the Latin-American kid hung in there, took his lumps and finally went down when several skillfully administered and lightning quick *shuto* chops slapped consciousness from his enraged mind.

A dozen years later, this same young gang member named Manuel Rivera, once again met Robert Falconi. Rivera was a Special Forces sergeant first class and Falconi a captain in the same elite outfit. SFC Manuel Rivera, a Black Eagle, was killed in action during the raid on the prison camp in North Vietnam in 1964. His name is now listed on the Black Eagles Roll of Honor.

When Falconi graduated from high school in 1952, he immediately enlisted in the Army. Although his father had wanted him to opt for West Point, the young man couldn't stand the thought of being stuck in any more classrooms. In fact, he didn't even want to be an officer. During his early days on army posts he had developed several friendships among career non-commissioned officers. He liked the attitude of these rough-and-tumble professional soldiers who drank, brawled and fornicated with wild abandon during their off-duty time. The sergeants' devil-may-care attitude seemed much more attractive to young Robert than the heavy responsibilities that seemed to make commissioned officers and their lives so serious and, at times, tedious.

After basic and advanced infantry training, he was shipped straight into the middle of the Korean War where he was assigned to the tough Second Infantry Division.

Falconi participated in two campaigns there. These were designated by the United States Army as: *Third Korean Winter* and *Korean Summer-Fall 1953.* Robert Falconi fought, roasted and froze in those turbulent months. His combat experience ranged from holding a hill during massive attacks by crazed Chinese Communist Forces, to the deadly cat-and-mouse activities of night patrols in enemy territory.

He returned stateside with a sergeancy, the Combat Infantryman's Badge, the Purple Heart, the Silver Star and the undeniable knowledge that he had been born and bred for just one life—that of a soldier.

His martial ambitions also had expanded. He now desired a commission but didn't want to sink himself into the curriculum of the United States Military Academy. His attitude toward schoolbooks remained the same—to hell with 'em!

At the end of his hitch in 1955, he re-enlisted and applied for Infantry Officers' Candidate School at Fort Benning, Georgia.

Falconi's time in OCS registered another success in

49

his life. He excelled in all phases of the rigorous course. He recognized the need for work in the classrooms and soaked up the lessons through long hours of study while burning the midnight oil of infantry academia in quarters. The field exercises were a piece of cake for this combat veteran, but he was surprised to find out that, even with his war experience, the instructors had plenty to teach him.

His only setback occurred during "Fuck Your Buddy Week." That was a phase of the curriculum in which the candidates learned responsibility. Each man's conduct—or misconduct—was passed on to an individual designated as his buddy. If a candidate screwed up he wasn't punished. His buddy was. Thus, for the first time in many of these young men's lives, their personal conduct could bring joy or sorrow to others. Falconi's "buddy" was late to reveille one morning and he drew the demerit.

But this was the only black mark in an otherwise spotless six months spent at OCS. He came out number one in his class and was offered a regular Army commission. The brand-new second lieutenant happily accepted the honor and set out to begin this new phase of his career in an Army he had learned to love as much as his father did.

His graduation didn't result in an immediate assignment to an active duty unit. Falconi found himself once more in school, but these were not filled with hours of poring over books. He attended jump school and earned the silver parachutists badge; next was ranger school where he won the coveted orange-and-black tab; then he was shipped down to Panama for jungle warfare school where he garnered yet one more insignia and qualification.

Following that he suffered another disappointment. Again, his desire to sink himself into a regular unit

50

was thwarted. Because he held a regular Army commission rather than a reserve one like his other classmates, Falconi was returned to Fort Benning to attend the Infantry School. The courses he took were designed to give him some thorough instruction in staff procedures. He came out on top here as well, but there was another thing that happened to him.

His intellectual side finally blossomed.

The theory of military science, rather than complete practical application, began to fascinate him. During his time in combat—and the later Army schooling—he had begun to develop certain theories. With the exposure to Infantry School, he decided to do something about these ideas of his. He wrote several articles for the *Infantry Journal* about these thoughts—particularly on his personal analysis of the proper conduct of jungle and mountain operations involving insurgency and counterinsurgency forces.

The Army was more than a little impressed with this first lieutenant (he had been promoted) and sent him back to Panama to serve on a special committee that would develop and publish U.S. Army policy on small-unit combat operations in tropical climates. He honed his skills and tactical expertise during this time.

From there he volunteered for Special Forces—the Green Berets—and was accepted. After completing the officers' course at Fort Bragg, North Carolina, Falconi was finally assigned to a real unit for the first time since his commission. This was the Fifth Special Forces Group in the growing conflict in South Vietnam.

He earned his captaincy while working closely with ARVN units. He even helped to organize village militias to protect hamlets against the Viet Cong and North Vietnamese. Gradually, his duties expanded until he organized and led several dangerous missions that involved deep penetration into territory controlled by the communist guerrillas.

It was after a series of these operations that he was linked up with the CIA officer Clayton Andrews. With their joint efforts the Black Eagles had been brought into existence, and it was as the commander of that unit that Lieutenant Colonel Robert Falconi now carried on his war against the communists.

Sixteen missions were now under his belt. There had been no medals, for such accolades are not for men who serve in clandestine, near illegal units that operate in the shadowy violence of highly classified operations. It had been bloody and heartbreaking, finally working its way to a point where he now sat in a rubber raft on the Gulf of Tonkin calmly rowing into what might be picking up a defector or looking into the AK47 muzzles of a commie trap!

Calcitra clunis, baby!

Chapter 5

General Truong Van put the two spare uniforms in his suitcase. After strapping it shut, he left his billet in the officers quarters and walked down the hall to the stairway. The young guard on duty there straightened into a position of attention as the general walked past him. Truong stopped at the reception desk. "Any messages?" he asked the clerk.

"Yes, Comrade General," the man answered. He reached into the distribution box and retrieved a piece of paper.

"Cam on ong," the general said. He walked outside and paused to read the note. It was to remind him of the appointment he had with the senior officer of the Hanoi Military Police District. Truong slipped it into his pocket and walked down to the curb where his car waited.

The driver smiled. *"Chao ong,* Comrade General."

Truong only grunted and got into the vehicle's back seat. When the driver slipped behind the steering wheel, the general gave his order in a curt voice. "Military Police Headquarters."

"Co, Comrade General!"

The driver lurched out into the street with his horn blaring. As a driver for a general, he was proud of the privileges he enjoyed when it came to traffic rules. Other vehicles, mostly bicycles and pedicabs, veered away as he recklessly wound his way through them.

Now and then a military officer or party official would dare to hold his own. But when they glanced into the car and saw Truong with the red badges edged in gold and bearing a single star on his collar, they quickly gave way. Then the young soldier-driver would grin broadly, lean on his horn and accelerate away.

Truong, however, was not enjoying the game. In fact, he was in a deeply sour mood. As proud and jealous of his rank as the driver, he hated the constant demands of his socialistic government's obsession with security. Many of the regulations concentrated more on the state's safety than they did on proper military protocol. It was bad enough having to put up with the KGB colonel attached to the Soviet embassy, but to have to report to a North Vietnamese colonel was doubly demeaning.

Truong enjoyed the sight of people scampering and turning away from his speeding vehicle. *"Mau len!"* he ordered. "Faster! Faster!"

The driver, happy to comply, sped up and now pounded madly on the horn button. Finally, with tires squealing, he wheeled around a corner and drew up to the curb, and slammed on the brakes.

"We are here, Comrade General," he announced. "Military Police Headquarters." He leaped out of the car and rushed around it to open the door.

Truong stepped from the car and hurried across the sidewalk, going directly into the building. He was in no mood for any bureaucratic nonsense from the clerk at the desk in the lobby. "Tell Comrade Colonel Minh that Comrade General Truong is here to see him."

The clerk, a civilian, enjoyed his own prestige. He liked to make high-ranking officers, who were usually quite nervous about being summoned to the military police, stew and wait. He smiled in a condescending manner. "I will see if the Comrade Colonel is—"

"Where is his office?" Truong interrupted.

"I must—"

"On your feet and take me to his office," Truong said. He reached across the desk and pulled the clerk toward him. "And be quick and happy about it."

The man swallowed with a nervous gulp. "Yes, Comrade General. Right away, Comrade General. Please release me, Comrade General." When he was free of Truong's grasp he motioned to him. "This way, Comrade General."

Truong followed the frightened man down a hallway. When they reached the door he didn't let the clerk knock. Instead, he pushed him aside and stepped into the office. "Comrade Colonel Minh!"

The colonel, as flustered as the clerk, leaped to his feet and saluted. "Yes? Yes, Comrade General?"

"I received a note stating I was to see you here at Military Police Headquarters," Truong said. He purposely avoided the phrase "report to you".

"Your name, Comrade General?" Minh asked nervously.

"Truong Van," the general answered.

The colonel quickly went through a wooden file box on his desk. "Yes. Yes. Here it is. Please sit down, Comrade General."

Truong lazily took a seat and pulled a cigarette from his tunic. He held it until the colonel scampered around to light it. Then he leisurely took a deep drag. "Let's get on with this."

"Of course, Comrade General," the colonel said. "We have received notice that you are leaving the Hanoi Military District. Is this so?"

"Of course!" Truong shouted. "I have been granted a furlough. I am going to the Army Rest Center at Ha Coi to relax a bit."

"Yes. Yes. All we need to do —according to regulations, Comrade General—is sign you out of this area," the colonel said. "A very simple thing, really."

"Fill out the form quickly and I will put my signature on it," Truong said.

The colonel scribbled in the information then slid it across the desk. "There. It is complete."

Truong wordlessly signed the document. Then he dropped the cigarette on the floor and ground it out with the heel of boot. The general left the office without another word and went back outside to his car.

The driver, smiling in delight, saluted. "Where now, Comrade General?"

"The rest center at Ha Coi," Truong said. "And let's see how fast this Russian automobile can travel."

"Co, Comrade General! *Co!"*

"Were there any notes?" Fagin asked the investigator.

"No, Chuck," the American MI officer answered. His name was Dan Reynolds and he was an old acquaintance of the CIA man. "As far as we can determine, Phuong had a few drinks, then went back to his office and blew his brains out."

Fagin stepped around Reynolds and walked up to the desk where Phuong's body was sprawled. He whistled softly. "You weren't kidding when you said he blew his brains out."

"Yeah. Real messy those .45s," Dan Reynolds said. He shrugged. "I wouldn't think it was a particularly unusual case. A lot of guys who have been through long captivity under the Reds commit suicide." He eyed Fagin closely. "So why was I called in here instead of the CID? We Military Intelligence boys aren't generally concerned when an ARVN colonel does a job on himself." He was thoughtful for several moments. "As a matter of fact, I don't know why our own Criminal Investigation Division would get involved." He sat down on the edge of the desk and lit a cigarette. "So level with me, Chuck. What's going down here?"

Fagin didn't answer right away. Instead he pulled a cigar from his jacket pocket. He didn't speak until he'd taken several long moments to light it. "I have an interest in the guy," Fagin said. "I wanted to pull a debrief on him about his time in the North Vietnamese slammer. When I heard he'd killed himself, I got curious. That's all."

"That's all?" Reynolds asked.

"Ain't that enough?"

"Not hardly, old buddy," Reynolds said. "Frankly I've got more to do than get called in to look at ARVN suicides. Why don't you check with his own army?"

Fagin chuckled. "Because I'd like some real information rather than have to pay bribes to some asshole who's not going to do anything but take my money and tell me things he thinks I want to hear."

Reynolds wasn't fooled. "You've already checked, haven't you? I'll bet the dossier on this guy told you nothing."

"Okay. I'm asking a favor. But if you don't come across, then I'll have to go through channels and you'll end up doing the work anyhow," Fagin said. "You've got no real need-to-know on the reasons behind the investigation. All I need is a thorough G2 look using all your assets and facilities." He paused and took a pull off his cigar. He eyed Reynolds. "The results of your work will go directly to General Taggart at SOG."

"Jesus!" Reynolds said.

"My own agency can't help," Fagin admitted. "But you MI types have your own turf. Maybe this guy

Phuong has spilled a little shit on it. We'd like to know."

"Okay, Chuck," Reynolds said. "I'll handle it personally. If there's anything at all, I promise to let you know."

"I appreciate that, Dan."

"By the way," Reynolds said. "How's my old pal Falconi?"

Fagin's expression was serious. "His ass is hanging on what you find out."

General Truong Van presented his furlough papers and identification card to the elderly civilian clerk at the Ha Coi Rest Center's reception desk. This was followed by a quick cross-checking of other papers. Finally, when everything tallied and matched up properly, the oldster was satisfied. "Please sign in, Comrade General," the civil servant said pushing the registration book toward him. "I hope your stay is relaxing and restful."

"*Cam on ong*, Comrade," Truong replied politely. "I assume my bungalow is fully prepared and stocked."

"Oh, yes, Comrade General," the old man said. "The accommodations are prepared per regulations for an officer of your rank." He pointed to a map on the wall. It showed the layout of the officers section of the rest camp. He indicated one particular spot. "There is your place, Comrade General. Very easy to find."

"There is liquor and other refreshments?" Truong asked.

"Of course, Comrade General."

"Fine." He checked his watch. "I will have a woman at ten o'clock."

"Yes, Comrade General," the elderly clerk said. "It will be arranged."

Truong's driver, who had been standing by the door, hurried forward and picked up the general's bag. "I know the way, Comrade General. I have brought other officers here." The soldier led the way out the door. They walked down a path canopied with palm trees. After making a turn, they stopped in front of a bungalow door. The driver pushed it open and stepped aside.

Truong stepped inside. There was one large room divided into a bedroom and living room. Another door on the far side led to a bathroom. Although the furniture was spartan in appearance, it seemed functional. A wet bar occupied one corner of the parlor area.

"Put the bag on the bed," Truong ordered.

The driver quickly complied. "Is there anything else, Comrade General?"

"No. You are dismissed."

"I shall return in one week," the man said.

"What?"

"I said, I shall be back to fetch you in a week, Comrade General."

"Yes. Yes. You are dismissed." Truong waited for the soldier to leave, then he went to the bar. A small refrigerator sat beneath it. He looked inside and found a bottle of orange juice. He took it and a liter of vodka, mixing a stiff drink. It tasted wonderful to him. Truong walked to the large window on the far side and looked out.

Two hundred meters away, he could easily see an army encampment. There were enough thatched huts laid out in symmetrical ranks and files to quarter a rifle battalion. He could see the troops quartered there. Although supposedly on rest status, they were engaged in classes and work details. Truong went

59

back to the bar to fix another drink.

A light rapping on the door interrupted him. "Yes?"

A young woman stepped inside. She was dressed in a Chinese dress with short sleeves and a tall collar that almost reached her chin. There were slits in the skirt, however, that went from the hemline to her upper thigh. She displayed a slight, polite smile. *"Chao ong,* Comrade General."

"Chao co," Truong said. "Would you care for a drink?"

"You are only allotted fifteen minutes, Comrade General," the young woman said. She checked the Russian watch on her wrist. "Then I am due to serve the comrade commissar in Bungalow Fourteen."

Truong nodded his understanding. He watched her walk over to the bed. Then he set his glass back on the bar and followed.

Andrea Thuy was worried. Her concern was so great that she made no attempt to hide it. Standing in the doorway of Chuck Fagin's office, she looked in at him and spoke firmly. "How good is this friend of yours?"

"Dan Reynolds?" Chuck mused. "I'd say he is about the best in the Saigon MI detachment."

"When do you expect his report?" Andrea wanted to know.

"In final form, in four of five days," Chuck said. "But he's already given me a preliminary verbal. In fact, I just got off the phone with him about ten minutes ago."

"The phone?" Andrea asked. "He used the phone to give out information?"

"There were no great secrets to divulge," Fagin said.

"This Colonel Phuong Bai was a real straight arrow. He earned his spurs with the French and has the *Croix de Guerre* with palms to prove it. They considered him a top-notch officer in their guerrilla campaigns. He knew the north damned good. That's why he was sent up there to run a net."

"Was he ever a prisoner during the time he fought with the French?" Andrea asked.

"No." Fagin answered. "He was first captured when the NVA policed him up about a year and a half ago."

Andrea sighed. "Then we don't have the slightest idea what he went through, do we? He could have turned on us, Chuck. He might have made a deal with the Reds to deliver Robert and the guys straight into their hands."

"That's a lot of supposing," Fagin said. "He says he managed to escape through this General Truong Van. According to Phuong, this general wanted to get to the south. The easiest way would be to have us pick him up and use our own transportation—air or sea—to get him down here. He trusted Phuong because the guy held tight under questioning." Fagin could see she was very worried, but he didn't want to let her know about his own misgivings. "Phuong was a hero, Andrea."

"Then why did he kill himself?" she asked.

Chuck didn't answer. He turned his head and stared out his window. "I don't know."

Chapter 6

Although Archie Dobbs had never been in that section of North Vietnam in his life, he moved toward the correct location of the link-up with unerring precision. All he needed was to be shown a point on the map to put into his own weirdly accurate perspective of direction, and he could move through the valleys, across ridge lines, and over hills as if he'd traveled the route countless times in his life.

Such a talent was as natural to Archie Dobbs as breathing. The young man was born a tracker and pathfinder.

If he had come into the world a couple of hundred years earlier, the intrepid corporal would have been among the first to break across the Appalachian or Allegheny Mountains. He would have been a companion of Daniel Boone, and his ilk during the great migrations west to explore the dangerous wilderness that spread out from the narrow seaboard of civilization. Archie would have loved to be the first to explore the unknown sprawl of the American continent. Archie's ancestors, who had arrived in the Colonies during the times when such activities were feasible, had been prevented from becoming pioneers because of the circumstances of their arrival.

They had come in chains, released from English prisons as bonded servants—virtual slaves to the people who held papers on them. Any attempt to leave the supervision and control of their masters was a serious crime. Confused and locked into a brutal system, they had no choice but to exist within the cruel mandates of the system. No man would want to escape even tyranny if it meant leaving his wife and children behind. In truth, they were as locked into slavery as the unfortunate blacks on southern plantations. After several generations, the former bonded servants, through circumstances brought on by the industrial revolution, were caught up in the manufacturing syndrome and life-style of the East Coast.

Thus, the Dobbs—like many other families—donated several generations to the mills and factories of Massachusetts.

Archie's older ancestors in England had been involved in more romantic activities to earn their bread. In fact, their way of making a living delivered them to the English judicial system that eventually sold the freebooting bunch into cruel bondage in the colonies.

The Dobbs family were poachers.

No earl, duke, lord of a manor, or even the King of England could keep the persistent Dobbs clan from hunting and fishing their private domains. Generations of following this dangerous trade had developed genes in which the necessary skills of stealth, tracking and directional orientation to the maximum. Fathers passed this unlawful trade down to their sons, until the craft seemed a part of their genetic heritage.

These talents were combined with stubbornness and fearlessness too.

To this day in the English county of Nottinghamshire a tale is told out of the misty past about a man named Crompton Dobbs who, rather than shrieking in agony while being drawn and quartered, shouted of how he had enjoyed the lord's roasted venison—the very crime for which he was being so painfully executed.

Now the scion of that great line of interloping outdoorsmen prowled through an enemy-infested tropical forest, looking for a stranger who would either add to the glory of the Black Eagle saga or end it in a treacherous ambush of betrayal and AK47 bullets.

Only two things kept Archie's pace down to a crawl. He was slowed because there was the need for absolute security. Dozens of NVA units scattered throughout the area. Although technically on rest status, they still maintained sentry and picket posts along with road blocks when necessary. The society that army served was not a free one. The government could not tolerate unrestricted commerce and travel by its citizenry.

The second problem Archie faced was darkness. This made it possible to follow trails rather than stumble through the thick vegetation to avoid visual discovery because the enemy could not see them. But this lack of good visibility meant that every noise or disturbance in the surrounding jungle, no matter how slight, had to be treated as if it were the harbinger of the arrival of the entire North Vietnamese Army. Archie had to signal for halts countless times. When this occurred, the detachment squatted down. Each man covered his area of firepower and security responsibility until the disturbance was checked out. Only after he was satisfied it was safe would Archie again beckon to his fellow Black Eagles to follow him.

The time dragged by slowly through the dreary hurry-up-and-wait routine until daylight began to loom across the jungle. It was a dull gray light at first, but gradually it grew brighter until visibility had almost doubled.

Once again Archie signaled a halt. This time the entire detachment moved off into the jungle. It was now too dangerous to attempt any further travel through this perilous area behind enemy lines. They would spend the daylight hours at this place, waiting once again for darkness to descend on them before moving out again for the uncertain rendezvous with the unknown NVA general.

The detachment walked slowly and carefully as they formed a tight circle. Then, at Top's whispered command, they settled down to make the position a defensive perimeter. This was SOP in the unit during times when they were forced into a long period of waiting while deep in enemy country. Every man prepared his locale as a combat site. Fields of fire were cleared away and the area in which they would lie was camouflaged.

The sleeping arrangements were for half the men to be awake at one time. That meant every other man would sleep for two hours, then be awakened to maintain watch while the other half of the detachment got some much needed rest.

Thus, hoping for the best but prepared for the worst, the Black Eagles settled in to pass the long daylight hours.

General Truong Van stretched out on the wicker lounging chair he'd placed in the shade behind his bungalow. A copy of one of the latest French novels lay open in his lap as he dozed peacefully in the hot weather. The NVA officer, knowing he had a physically demanding task ahead of himself, had been eating and resting as much as possible in preparation for the ordeal.

He'd just begun to slip into a deep sleep when the voice of an orderly broke into his restfulness.

"Comrade General?"

Irritated, but controlling his temper, Truong turned and looked at the man standing in the back door. *"Cai nay la cai gi?"*

"You have a caller, Comrade General," the orderly said apologetically. "It is a Russian colonel named Sogolov."

"Merde!" Truong swore in French. But he got up, carrying his book with him as he followed the orderly into the bungalow. He saw Sogolov standing by the bar. "Hello, Comrade Colonel."

"And greetings to you, Comrade General," Sogolov said. "I see you are reading a book. Is it good?"

"It is on the bestseller list in Paris," Truong answered.

"I suggest you try some of our Russian novelists," Sogolov said. "They are the finest in the world." He was the next-to-senior Soviet KGB officer stationed in Hanoi at that particular moment. He had not been in Southeast Asia long, and had yet to adapt himself to the weather. Sweat streamed down his face and soaked his khaki uniform. He was clearly uncomfortable. "May I fix myself a drink?"

"Of course, Comrade Colonel," Truong said. He walked over and sat down on one of the room's two chairs.

Sogolov took a glass and filled it with vodka. He drank it all down in a few gulps. "This is the only thing that helps me bear up under this heat."

"Please," Truong said. "Have another."

The Russian gratefully poured himself one more glassful. He went to the remaining chair and sat down. "This is a nice place."

"Yes," Truong agreed. "Most restful."

"I didn't realize you were in need of a vacation," Sogolov said pleasantly. "At least you said nothing to me."

Truong smiled. "I suppose it never came up in casual conversation."

"One would hope such revelations would be part of official courtesy," Sogolov said. "After all, you've worked closely with the KGB in Hanoi for the past several years. We like to keep tabs on our special friends."

"I don't suppose I considered myself that important," Truong said. "I am only a North Vietnamese general, hardly worth a second thought to a Russian colonel."

Sogolov did not miss the sarcasm in the general's remarks. But he made no outward sign that he was upset. "Actually, I was a bit concerned about you. I thought you might be feeling badly about the prisoner who escaped your custody."

"Do you mean the South Vietnamese colonel?" Truong asked. "Let me think—what was his name?"

"Phuong," Sogolov said knowing damned well that Truong knew who he was talking about. "Colonel Phuong Bai."

"I don't believe he actually escaped *my* custody, Comrade Colonel," Truong said. "He was in the company of a major and driver at the time. Somehow he got the officer's pistol and killed both men. Then he disappeared."

"How do you suppose he managed that?" Sogolov said.

"I would imagine he grabbed the pistol when the major grew careless," Truong said. "One must stay alert when escorting or guarding prisoners."

"Indeed," Sogolov said. "But actually I was wondering how the colonel was able to evade capture and return to South Vietnam."

"Did he?" Truong said. "I really hadn't much interest in the case."

"Colonel Phuong Bai was even decorated by his decadent government," Sogolov said. "Then he committed suicide."

"How strange," Truong said. "Perhaps he was a bit unbalanced. After all, our forms of imprisonment and examination is not designed to promote mental health, are they?"

Sogolov finished the vodka and leaned forward. "I was wondering, Comrade General, if you have any special programs or operations in force at this time."

"Oh, no, Comrade Colonel," Truong said. "I would certainly inform the KGB if I did."

"Are you sure that you don't have something in that works that you should be sharing with your Soviet brothers?"

Rage welled up in Truong like a bellowing volcano, but he kept his demeanor calm and cool. "Of course not, Comrade Colonel." He pointed to his unwelcome companion's glass. "Why don't you get yourself another drink?"

But Sogolov shook his head. "Not now, Comrade General." He stood up. "But I shall return to enjoy some more of your vodka. Good day to you."

"Good day to you, Comrade Colonel," Truong said.

The day eased slowly through its hours for the Black Eagles. Concealed in the jungle vegetation, they felt insidious heat sinking into their position like an invisible cloud of steam. Soaked in perspiration, they alternated through the sleep-guard routine, sipping the lukewarm water from their canteens and nibbling at the cans of fruit in their C-rations. Anything heavier seemed unappetizing.

The command post was no more than a small hollow in the ground bordered by fallen trees that had died and crashed to the mushy ground years before. Lieutenant Colonel Robert Falconi and First Lieutenant Ray Swift

Elk sat side-by-side, resting against one of the rotting trunks.

"We didn't have much time to discuss any contingencies," Swift Elk said. He noted the sinking sun. "It's kind of silly to bring it up at this late date, I guess."

"Not really," Falconi said. "Things in this operation are going to be real simple no matter what happens. If the mission comes off as planned, we'll be back drinking beer in our bunker at Nui Dep within twenty-four hours."

Swift Elk grinned. "Unless we can talk General Taggart into giving the guys some time off in Saigon."

"Don't count on it," Falconi said. He continued. "However, should this turn out to be a betrayal, we'll have no choice but to haul ass."

"Jesus, sir! We're almost on the Chinese border!"

"Right," Falconi said. "Logic would dictate that we head south." He glanced around, then lowered his voice. "Of course, nobody would expect us to go north into Red China, would they?"

"You have something special in mind, don't you, sir?" Swift Elk asked.

"I don't want to bring it out now," Falconi said. "In case we lose some guys as prisoners, there's no sense in having them be able to tell our plans." He turned his glance to the open box of C-rations sitting beside Swift Elk. "Speaking of plans, Lieutenant, do you have any special ones for that pound cake?"

Before he could answer, Archie Dobbs stepped into the command post. "It's getting late afternoon, sir. Just about time to move off for the meet."

"Do you remember the exact location?" Falconi asked.

"You bet," Archie answered. He pulled out his map. Although it was unmarked in case it fell into enemy hands, he put his finger on the exact point. "There's a small rocky hill just south of that creek. That's where our general will be."

"That's where he's *supposed* to be," Swift Elk corrected him.

"Well," Archie conceded. "It'll either be him or a battalion of North Vietnamese infantry."

"Your casual acceptance of *karma* is really Oriental, Archie," Swift Elk said grinning.

"Yeah," Archie said. "Maybe I've been out here in Southeast Asia too long."

"Maybe we all have," Falconi said. "Now what about the challenge and password?"

"Whoever gets in close to the guy says, 'Hot'," Archie replied. "For his sake, he'd better come back with 'Potato.' If not, the population of the People's Socialist Republic of North Vietnam is going to go down by one."

"If it isn't the guy we're looking for, let's just hope whoever it is will be alone," Swift Elk interjected.

"That's why we're going to run one hell of a recon on the contact area," Falconi said. "If there are any nasty surprises, I want us to have at least a running chance to break loose and get the hell out of there."

Top Gordon climbed over the fallen trees marking the command post. "The detachment is all formed up and ready to move out, sir," he reported.

"Let's get the show on the road then," Falconi said. He winked at the sergeant major. "It's now or never."

"Now or never," Top said repeating the words. Then he added, "Or over forever."

"You're a poet," Falconi said.

"I'm a fucking realist, sir," Top said. He saluted then went back over the trees to join the column.

70

Chapter 7

The orderly picked up the plate holding the remnants of the melon. "Will there be anything else, Comrade General?"

"Is there liquor in the cabinet?" Truong Van asked.

The orderly nodded. "Yes, Comrade General. I have just inspected the quantity myself. There is Russian vodka and Cuban rum."

"*Cam on ong*," Truong said. "I have much work to do tonight and I do not wish to be disturbed."

"Yes, Comrade General," the orderly said. "Do you not wish for me to dispatch a woman to you?"

"I do not," Truong said. "I also will not require breakfast in the morning. I do not think my task will be finished much before daylight. Therefore I shall sleep until mid-day."

"*Co*, Comrade General." The man bowed, then made a hasty withdrawal.

Truong went into the bedroom and pulled his suitcase from under the bed. Opening it, he withdrew a pistol belt that held the Russian Tokarev pistol and canteen. After making sure all was in order, he inspected the dark green field uniform and boots. He slipped out of the light garrison tunic and trousers, and put on the combat clothing. After donning the boots and lacing them securely, he went back to the living room carrying the pistol belt with him. He sat down on the chair there and lit a cigarette, smoking leisurely.

Truong had no intention of touching the liquor in the bungalow. His planned activities for that night would require a sharp mind, physical coordination, and the possibility of life-or-death decisions to be made in a matter of split seconds.

Instead of drinking, he smoked heavily. Lighting one cigarette on the dying embers of another, the North Vietnamese general had a thick cloud of smoke hanging around his head. In spite of a raw throat and irritated nostrils, he consumed the contents of two full packs of cigarettes in a three-hour period. Now and then he would get to his feet and pace back and forth across the room. The only refreshment he allowed himself was an occasional drink of water at the wet bar.

The phone in the room rang. Truong picked it up. "*A-lo,*" he said.

"The time is 2300 hours, Comrade General," said the voice on the other end.

"Yes. Thank you," Truong said. He hung up. The call was not a courtesy afforded the guests of the rest center. Instead it was a thinly veiled roll call to make sure everyone was where he was supposed to be. It would be the final one until five o'clock in the morning. The general took a final drag on his cigarette and crushed it out in the mounds of butts in the overflowing ashtray.

It was now safe to go.

Truong turned off all the lights, then went to the rear door. He peered outside and waited to make sure there was no one near to hear or see him. When he was satisfied it was safe, he eased through the flimsy portal and tip-toed across the small patio to the back wall. Again he spent a few moments listening. He could

72

perceive nothing but the sounds of night insects whirring through the nearby jungle. Truong reached up to the top of the wall and deftly hauled himself up. Lying flat to make a low silhouette, he slipped over and dropped silently to the ground. After a few moments to once again make sure he'd not been spotted, Truong walked in a low crouch along a path leading into the monsoon forest. Once he was in the tree line, he stood erect and walked swiftly but silently along the trail he'd already scouted.

The general knew every step of the way. When he reached a point where he knew a sentry post was located, he slowed down and continued toward it in an alert manner. Truong was forced to come to a complete halt when he reached it. The sentry was making his rounds and, as luck would have it, had reached the point where the general now waited in the darkness. Truong bided his time until the guard walked away to the other end of his post. Then, once again moving rapidly, he crossed the secured area and went deeper into the jungle.

Truong continued on for an hour. The clinging, thick brush forced his movement in the dark to a maddeningly slow pace. But finally he could hear the sound of rapidly running water. Fifteen more meters and he stood on the bank of a shallow creek. He waded in and quickly crossed it, turning slightly to the north.

Another half hour brought him to his destination. A rocky hill loomed up ahead of him. He skirted the formation of boulders to the other side. Finally he was able to stop.

Truong squatted in the darkness to wait.

Archie Dobbs signaled a halt. He sat silently for

73

several moments, then spoke into his Prick Six. "Falcon, this is Arch. We're in the area now. Over."

"Roger. Out," came the reply.

Top Gordon, who had monitored the transmission, went into action. He made sure the men had formed a tight position that would throw out the maximum fire power if they blundered into a trap. He stayed in the center of the perimeter. Falconi and Ray Swift Elk joined him.

"We've got to give this area a good going-over," Falconi said. "I want Ray and Paulo Garcia to check out the south side."

"Yes, sir," Ray Swift Elk said. "I'll pick up Paulo on the perimeter."

"Right," Falconi said. He nudged Top. "I want Malpractice and Blue to pull a recon to the north."

"Yes, sir," Top said. "What about the rest of the guys?"

"I'm going to take Archie west with me to make the contact," Falconi said. "You stay here with the remainder and watch the east. In case this thing turns to shit, that'll be our only way out of here and back to the coast and the submarine."

"We'll give that duty our best efforts," Top said with a wry grin. "Don't worry, sir."

"Okay. Now listen up, Sergeant Major," Falconi said. "If this is a set-up, you're going to hear some real loud shooting. That'll be the signal for everyone to head for the coast. You'll take the main body with you. I don't want any heroics, understand?"

"Yes, sir," Top said.

"You just keep moving," Falconi said. "That'll do the rest of us the most good. We can follow in your wake if you've cleared a path for us. Any rear-guard actions will only slow us up, and give the NVA more time to surround the detachment."

74

"Understood, sir," the sergeant major assured the Black Eagle commander. "What about the other patrols—Ray, Paulo, Malpractice, and Blue?"

"Tell 'em to haul ass too," Falconi said. "Get to it." He paused. "If the submarine shows up, then the guys that are on the beach go aboard. Anybody who's late gets left behind. That includes me." He poked the sergeant major's shoulder to emphasize his point. "That is a goddamned, bona fide direct order from your commanding officer!"

Top nodded. "I realize the importance of not getting us all policed up if possible, sir. Don't worry. I'll do my duty." He turned away and went to the perimeter. Ray Swift Elk followed him and grabbed Paulo Garcia by the shoulder. "C'mon, Gyrene. The old man wants us to check out the action to the south."

"How about as far south as Saigon?" Paulo asked with a grin.

"No such luck," Ray said. "The best I can possibly do for you is about a hundred meters. I'll give you the rest of the poop on this phase of the mission while we move out of here."

Top didn't watch the pair leave. Instead he rounded up Malpractice McCorckel and Blue Richards. "You two guys are gonna pull a recon on the north side of this place. Keep a low profile and remember not to engage the enemy if at all possible."

"Can we spit in their eye?" Blue asked.

"No," Top growled. "And you can't piss on their shoes neither. Now listen up! While you're sneakin'-and-peekin', the old man and Archie are gonna move forward to make the contact. If ever'thing's on the up-and-up, you oughta be able to get back here at the same time they do."

Malpractice was a practical non-commissioned officer. That meant he was a natural pessimist. "What if

75

things are all fucked up?" he bluntly asked.

"Then you're gonna hear a lot of yelling and shooting," Top said. "That's your signal to head east as fast as your legs will carry you. Me and the rest of the guys are gonna open up a path all the way to the coast. Fall in behind us and run like hell."

"Ain't we gonna stop and slow up the NVA?" Blue asked.

"Negative," Top said. "We hit the coast and look for the submarine. Once it's there, the guys that are all present and accounted for go for it. Anybody that ain't there gets left behind."

"Shit!" Blue swore.

"Don't make with the comments," Top said. "Get out on that recon!"

Meanwhile, on the west side of the operation, Falconi and Archie Dobbs moved slowly through the woods. They would have liked to exercise even more caution, but time was already running out. Archie suddenly stopped and grabbed Falconi's arm. "There it is, sir!"

They could see the rocky hill ahead. Bathed in the moonlight, the boulders glistened slightly as if luminescent. Falconi glanced around. "Let's take the long route."

"I'm with you," Archie said.

They took a circuitous route until they drew close. Falconi spoke out in a normal tone of voice. "Sneaking around is over, Archie. Let's see if this mission is for real."

They moved forward, exposing themselves to any ambush that might be waiting for them. Suddenly a figure seemed to rise out of the darkness. It stood motionless, waiting.

Falconi licked his lips. "Hot—," he said.

"—Potato," came the reply.

76

The two Black Eagles walked up to the man. "General Truong Van?" Falconi asked.

"Yes," Truong said. "I am ready to leave with you."

Archie Dobbs reached out and grabbed the general's arm. "C'mon," he said. "Next stop Saigon."

The NVA driver pulled the small Soviet UAZ-69A command car up to the front of the Ha Coi Army Rest Center's reception building. He quickly got out into the cool dawn air and opened the door for his passenger, KGB Colonel Dimitri Sogolov.

"Wait here," Sogolov instructed him. "I shall return promptly with the comrade general."

He went into the building and flashed his special identity card at the clerk there. "I am here to see Comrade General Truong," the Russian announced.

"I am sorry, Comrade Colonel," the man on duty said. "The comrade general left word he would be sleeping late this morning."

Sogolov ignored the man as he went through the side door and walked rapidly toward the VIP bungalows. There had been an exciting message received in Hanoi only a couple of hours before. Communist operatives in Saigon had radioed a terse but informative broadcast informing the Red brass that Lieutenant Colonel Robert Falconi and his Black Eagle Detachment had disappeared from South Vietnam. They were not at Peterson Field or Camp Nui Dep. All that was known was that they'd passed through Saigon and then moved on some place else. Anytime that happened, the intelligence offices went into overtime to monitor communications, read field reports, and check out rumors—anything—that might give away the location and activities of Falconi's gangsters.

He stopped at Truong's bungalow and banged on

the door. "Comrade General! Comrade General!" There was no answer. He beat on the portal again, then finally kicked it open. The KGB officer stormed inside. "Are you asleep? What—"

Sogolov looked around the empty two rooms. He noted the ashtray and the enormous pile of cigarette butts in it. The colonel walked to the back door and out onto the patio. He could see a slight disturbance of the vines on the rear wall. He checked them out, then pulled himself on the top. He could see the ground on the other side where a set of boot tracks led off into the jungle.

The full realization hit the Russian.

He shook with rage and clenched his fists so hard the fingernails dug into the palms of his hands. "That little slant-eyed son of a bitch!" Sogolov hissed in fury. "He has defected!"

Chapter 8

Calvin Culpepper and Blue Richards pulled the branches off the raft and wrestled the craft out of the tree line and onto the beach.

Falconi, with more to do than supervise that particular chore, left the physical preparation of the exfiltration to Sergeant Major Top Gordon. The lieutenant colonel, with his Prick-Six radio up to his mouth, spoke tersely into the instrument:

"Moby Dick, this is Falcon. Over."

The only sound he heard in the receiving end was the hissing of dead air.

"Moby Dick. Moby Dick, this is Falcon. Over."

Ray Swift Elk, standing beside him, was listening on his own radio. "Damn! If they've missed the rendezvous we're in deep shit."

"Yeah," Falconi agreed. He tried again. "Moby Dick. Moby Dick, this is Falcon. Over. I say again. Moby Dick, this is Falcon. Over."

Another few moments of empty air followed, but suddenly a voice broke through. They recognized the voice of the submarine *Perch*'s skipper. "Falcon, this is Moby Dick. Over."

Falconi grinned. "Moby Dick, we are ready for the pick-up," the Black Eagle commander said. Then he added the code words that only he and the submarine captain knew. "Jump on it." This phrase let the sub skipper know that everything was fine and there were no slipups. "This is Falcon. And we'll be glad to be back aboard. Over."

The submarine radioed back. "Roger. Let's do it. Out."

Falconi gave a thumbs-up signal to Sergeant Major Gordon. "It's time to get out of here."

"Yes, sir!" Top said. He turned to the men. "Okay, guys. Port and starboard, man the boat."

The detachment split into two groups, taking the same rowing positions they had when they left the submarine. Each man, with his rifle slung across his back, grabbed a paddle with one hand and one of the raft's carrying handles with the other.

"Into the water," Top ordered. "And make it quick."

"Flank speed, y'all," Blue Richards hollered happily.

They ran into the low surf with Falconi and General Truong Van following. When the water was deep enough, they all jumped in. Falconi allowed the NVA general to precede him and occupy a spot in the middle of the small craft. Then the detachment commander leaped into his regular coxswain's position where he would steer the rubber boat.

"Stroke! Stroke!" he called out marking the cadence for the rowers. "Port around starboard! Now give way together! Stroke!"

The Black Eagles' muscular arms worked rhythmically as they dug the paddles into the water and pulled hard against the force of the ocean. They kept at the task until a sudden disturbance in the water three hundred meters ahead created splashing foam that glistened in the moonlight. Then the conning tower of the submarine shot out of the ocean amidst the disturbance.

Falconi, so startled that he forgot his nautical commands, shouted, "Whoa!" He didn't want to chance any violent collisions with the submarine when it came up from the depths.

Chuckling to themselves, the Black Eagles immediately stopped rowing and set the paddles across their legs.

"Hey, that's the bus home," Top said laughing.

"Then row, you bastards!" Falconi said in a good humor. "Stroke! Stroke! Goddamn it! Stroke!"

Now laughing in relief and joy at completing their mission, the Black Eagles worked harder than ever. The rubber raft seemed to lift itself as it traveled across the water toward the conning tower of the *Perch*.

Suddenly bright lights lit up the scene. Falconi at first thought it was a spotlight from the submarine, but he quickly saw it came from the near horizon. Spurts of water leaped up around the boat. Archie Dobbs spoke an understatement that summed up the situation both accurately and completely:

"Damn! We're under fire!"

A North Vietnamese patrol boat, its heavy machine gun belching flame and bullets, roared into the vicinity. Now the noise of the weapon could be heard as its "chuga-chuga" threw out tracer slugs that sliced like laser beams through the night air.

The commander of the *Perch*, now fully aware of the situation, had no choice. Both military doctrine and orders dictated what he must do. The submarine sank beneath the waves with the same abrupt intensity it had appeared.

"Plan Red!" Falconi shouted.

Paulo Garcia suddenly reached over and grabbed General Truong Van by the collar. He pulled the NVA officer over the side and into the sea with him. Then, still holding on to the struggling man, he swam toward the shore using powerful strokes. Weighted down with both the defector and his gear, it took all of Paulo's strength to swim even in the direction of the ocean's movement toward the shore.

The men forward in the raft had already pulled the M16s off their backs. They cut loose on full automatic at the spotlight of the patrol boat. Sparks showed in the dark where the slugs ricocheted off the craft's sides, but suddenly its light went out.

There was a brief cheer from the Black Eagles, but it was quickly choked off when another enemy boat appeared. Falconi, like the submarine captain, had little to choose from in the way of alternate action. "Into the water," he bellowed. "We'll meet on the beach. Until then, it's every man for himself."

They slipped overboard and began clumsily swimming in their gear. None had trouble staying underwater to avoid detection by the enemy patrol boat. They only surfaced long enough to grab lungfuls of air before going back under the waves and continuing toward the beach.

It took ten agonizing minutes before they finally reached the surf where they'd be safe from the North Vietnamese craft. When the detachment reached the beach, they wasted no time in running across the sand and into the tree line.

Top Gordon, one of the first in, had found Paulo and Truong. After positioning them, he began to gather up the others. The last man in was Malpractice McCorckel. He was coughing and hacking from swallowing so much sea water. Top checked him out, then helped him over to the rest of the group.

Falconi, soaking wet like the others, surveyed his men. He glanced dully at Truong, then back at them. "The situation," he announced, "has gone to shit."

Chuck Fagin's ringing phone broke through the whiskey-drenched sleep he'd slipped into so deeply. Still a bit drunk, he got the receiver off the hook and laid it on his pillow. "Yeah?"

The voice coming out of the telephone was unintelligible at that distance from his ear. But its persistent yammering finally brought him to wakefulness. He picked up the instrument. "Fagin here."

"You sleepy sonofabitch!" came General James Taggart's bellowing voice. "Get your Irish ass down here."

"Something going on, huh?" Fagin said.

"Yeah. And it's all bad news. Move it, Fagin!"

Fagin, his head now buzzing with an awful hangover, stumbled out of the bed and lurched across the room to where his clothes were scattered all over the floor. Knowing full well that the information Taggart had for him involved the Black Eagles, he tried to hurry up. But all he accomplished was to get more mixed up and tumble to the floor while trying to pull on his trousers.

"Okay. Okay," he said to himself. "Let's gather our wits, shall we, Fagin? Slow and easy, that's the ticket. Slow and easy."

He began to dress in a methodical, logical manner. It took him ten minutes, but when he'd finished, he was completely and properly prepared to go down to SOG headquarters. He left his apartment and went down to the secured parking area of the complex where he lived. He had been issued a regulation jeep some weeks previously, and loved the tough little vehicle. He started it up and headed for the gate. After clearing himself with the South Vietnamese guard there, he drove like crazy through the streets of Saigon.

His arrival at Peterson Field included a slow and frustrating I.D. check by M.P.s, but he finally got past them and went up to Taggart's office.

The general didn't waste time in hemming and hawing. "The Black Eagles have been compromised," he announced.

Fagin, more of an intelligence specialist than the general, was prone to show more caution before making any judgments on the situation. "What's happened?"

"The meet with the sub went off as planned," Taggart said. "Then two North Vietnamese patrol boats showed up and spoiled everything. They fired directly into the Black Eagles' raft."

"Casualties?"

"The sub skipper doesn't know," Taggart said. "He took a quick look through his periscope and saw the guys in their raft. The next instant it was empty. Draw your own conclusion."

"Was the North Vietnamese general with them?"

"We're damned sure he was," Taggart said. "Falconi gave the code words that all was well before the sub surfaced."

"Those patrol boats could have come across the exfiltration by accident," Fagin said. "If their general was in the boat, he would be pretty stupid to arrange for a couple of speedy craft to show up blasting away in his vicinity."

84

"Maybe he figured it was worth it," Taggart said. "And maybe it wasn't the general."

"It could have been a set-up by some fanatic," Fagin agreed. He pulled out a cigar and lit up. "Well, I'm going to be stuck here monitoring what's going on. I'd better give Andrea a call. She'll want to sweat this out with me."

"Fagin," Taggart said sincerely. "I really hope they come back."

"Yeah. Me too."

"We're going to be up to our eyeballs in NVA within an hour," Archie Dobbs said to Lieutenant Colonel Robert Falconi.

"I wouldn't disagree on that point," Falconi said. He glanced over at General Truong standing beside him. "Do you know any real good shortcuts out of here?"

Truong nodded. "I have an E&E net that leads to the south," he said helpfully.

"You run an escape and evasion net toward South Vietnam?" Falconi asked. "Who for?"

"I have conducted some missions in the past that I did not wish to discuss in great detail with the Soviet KGB. Also, I had planned to use it myself in the event that I found it prudent to leave North Vietnam."

Falconi eyed him closely. "Why didn't you use it to defect?"

"It would take too long," Truong explained. "When I finally decided to go, I had a few things to clear up. It seemed the smart thing to do to send Colonel Phuong through the net to make sure I received the right reception."

"But we can't use it," Falconi protested. "Don't you think your agents would become a trifle suspicious if nine Americans suddenly appeared in one of their safehouses?"

"They are well-trained and blindly obedient," Truong said. He smiled slightly. "Good communists, hey?"

"You say this net is to the south?" Falconi asked.

"Yes, Colonel," Truong answered.

Falconi motioned to Archie. "We'll be heading due north."

"North!" Truong exclaimed. "That is Red China!"

"I want Mao's autograph," Falconi said. "Move out, Archie!"

"Yes, sir!"

The detachment formed up with Archie on the point followed by Blue Richards. Falconi, Swift Elk, and their guest of honor General Truong Van were in the center. Top Gordon and Gunnar Olson brought up the rear while Calvin and Malpractice were set out as flankers on each side of the column.

They moved as rapidly as possible through the jungle until the dawn made its scarlet appearance through the eastern tree line. After a half hour more of the movement, it was bright enough for Falconi to begin thinking about settling in for the day.

That's when they stumbled into the North Vietnamese patrol.

The firefight broke out immediately in the front. The NVA, a unit of veterans, blasted straight out ahead of them. Archie Dobbs and Blue Richards had no choice but to dive for cover. They huddled close to the ground while bullets clipped twigs and leaves just above their heads.

86

Archie, his face pressed flat into the soft jungle terrain, laboriously pulled his M16 into position where he could fire it. He made a quick effort, but had to duck back down as a heavy volley of incoming fire smacked in the empty air above him.

"Cool it, Archie," Blue said from just behind him. "We ain't gonna be able to git outta here on our own. The other boys will have to do it for us."

"You ain't lying!" Archie agreed as the shooting toward their positions increased.

Farther back, the other Black Eagles tried to lessen the pressure on their two buddies. They charged forward in leaps and bounds, practicing fire-and-maneuver as they edged closer to the enemy position. But the crescendo of enemy fusillades rose to a continuous, ear-deafening roar, forcing them to pull back.

Calvin Culpepper, however, wasn't the kind of guy to leave his buddies in the lurch. He broke loose from the main body and managed to make a wide circle around to the rear of the enemy. When he was in the right spot, he launched a yelling, full-automatic, one-man attack.

Startled, the NVA turned to meet this unexpected assault. They had no sooner responded when another similar one hit them from the other side. This time it was Malpractice McCorckel. His action forced the confused Reds to shift all their fire toward the rear.

Falconi, correctly judging the situation, didn't waste any time. "Let's go!"

The frontal charge was renewed. He led Top, Ray, and Gunnar into the fray. The only man who stayed back was Paulo Garcia who had been saddled with watching General Truong Van.

The Black Eagle attack swept over Blue and Archie. They leaped up and joined in as their skirmish line crashed into the NVA unit. The fight broke down into a brief, swirling massacre as the surrounded North Vietnamese were swept away in the coordinated volleys of Falconi's men.

Suddenly it was over.

The stillness seemed strange after the thundering activity of moments before. The Black Eagles stood among the corpses of the dead NVA.

Falconi glanced over at Archie. "What the hell are you waiting for? Didn't I tell you I wanted Mao Tse Tung's autograph?"

"You bet, sir," Archie replied. He motioned to the others. "Follow me, men. I'm off to show you Red China—home of egg rolls, chow mein, and the world's biggest goddamned army!"

Chapter 9

The sun's rays burned in through the openings in the canopy of tall palm trees. The jungle had grown mute and still in the afternoon heat. Even the insects seemed to be taking a siesta in the stifling weather.

The Black Eagles, along with their guest General Truong Van, had situated themselves down in a hollow where it was at least a bit cooler. Although no breeze freshened up the atmosphere, the shade was deeper and more intense. Most of the activity was simply staying on the alert and listening for any sounds of intruders. Four of the Black Eagles—Falconi, Archie Dobbs, Ray Swift Elk, and Top Gordon—huddled around a map making a paper reconnaissance of the route they intended to follow up to Red China. They spoke in soft murmurs, aligning their compasses with the magnetic north indicator on the military topographical chart.

Paulo Garcia, acting as the detachment intelligence specialist, was the only other man doing something active. He searched through his patrol pack and finally pulled out a small packet. He walked over to General Truong and squatted down beside him. "Let's make a fingerprint check, General."

"I was wondering when that was going to happen," Truong said with a slight smile.

"Did you know we had a set of yours on file?" Paulo asked.

"Of course," Truong answered. "They were taken

from a glass I used at the Hungarian Embassy. A Vietnamese servant there was an operative for your side. He sent them down to your intelligence people."

"How did you find that out?"

"The man told us much under interrogation," Truong said.

"I'll bet he did," Paulo said. "Let's get this over with, General."

Truong held out his hand and allowed the U.S. Marine to ink his fingertips and press them down on a card especially designed and printed for that purpose. He took time to light a cigarette, then offered the other hand. Paulo did the job quickly and professionally, producing good readable copies of prints.

"Thank you," Paulo said. He carefully packed away his gear and took the results of his work over to First Lieutenant Ray Swift Elk. The Sioux Indian had been through the most advanced of the U.S. Army's intelligence schools and training courses. One large block of this instruction was a series of classes entitled "EEFIS." The acronym stood for Escape and Evasion Fingerprint Identification System. The purpose of this system was to identify persons put into Escape and Evasion nets set up by Special Forces troops operating behind enemy lines.

If an American pilot was shot down and lucky enough to both avoid capture and get policed up by a Green Beret "A" Detachment, the unit's intelligence sergeant would make a set of fingerprints of the aviator. Then, using a special code, a description of the prints would be broadcast back to the Special Forces Operational Base where the data would be compared with the pilot's fingerprints on file. Once it was confirmed that the man was a real, live, true-blue American Air Force officer, the Green Berets would insert him into their Escape and Evasion Net to be transported out of enemy territory and back through friendly lines. Within a short time, if all went well, the pilot would be back flying missions against the bad guys.

But, on the other hand, if an individual showed up in enemy territory making claim to being a member of the U.S. armed forces and his fingerprints didn't match those in his records, those same helpful Special Forces guys would sweat the real truth out of him. Then, likely as not, he'd end up a bullet-pocked cadaver in some lonely, unmarked grave.

EEFIS is serious business.

Ray Swift Elk and Paulo Garcia drew off from the main group to tend to the important task ahead. They put the freshly made fingerprints side by side with the photocopies of Truong's that were on file with the Central Intelligence Agency and U.S. Army Military Intelligence. Using a five-power magnifier, Swift Elk looked at each one of the prints, comparing it with its fresh counterparts. When he'd finished, he handed the stuff over to Paulo. "It's all yours."

"Aye, aye, sir," Paulo said. He performed the same chore, taking his time as he made minute, painstaking studies. When he was finished, he nodded. "We got the right guy."

"Yeah," Swift Elk agreed. "That is undoubtedly General Truong Van."

The two wasted no time in reporting in to their detachment commander. "He's the real McCoy, sir," Swift Elk said.

"Them prints match up perfectly," Paulo added.

"Okay," Falconi said. "I've seen the dossier on the guy. There's one more thing left to do." He left the others and walked over to the general who was squatting Oriental style as he chain-smoked. Falconi sat down on the ground beside him. "How are you doing, General?"

91

"Quite well, thank you, Colonel," Truong said. "I trust my fingerprints passed with flying colors."

"Indeed," Falconi said. Then he quickly said in Russian, "It's always hot this time of the year, *nyet?*"

"*Da,*" Truong replied. "*Vsegda posle o dozhde.*" He smiled, then continued to speak in the language of the Soviet Union. "It is true what we have heard. You speak Russian fluently and without an American accent."

"I suppose you know why," Falconi remarked dryly.

"Could it be because your mother is Russian?" Truong asked. "Surely you learned the language from her as you learned English from your father."

Falconi stood up. "I'll leave that to your own conclusions."

"Of course," Truong said. "Have I now passed all the tests?"

"I am convinced you are General Truong Van," Falconi said unemotionally. "But I warn you. If this is a ploy to compromise or destroy this detachment, you'll never see the end result. I'll kill you myself."

Truong displayed a slight, patient smile. "Perhaps I am willing to give up my life in order to bring about the destruction of the Black Eagles."

"That's exactly what it will take," Falconi said coldly. He went back to his map conference.

Truong, still smiling, lit another cigarette.

The chief of the Hanoi military police nervously shuffled the papers before sliding them across the desk to the Russian KGB colonel who sat opposite him. "All the information is here, Comrade Colonel."

"Thank you," Dimitri Sogolov said. "And I appreciate having it translated into Russian."

"That is standard procedure," the military police officer said. "Are you ready to see the investigator now?"

"Yes. Thank you."

The military policeman went to the door and opened it. "Lieutenant Ahn, *moi ong vao.*"

A young North Vietnamese officer made an appearance. He was a tough-looking, thorough sort of man. His manner was matter-of-fact and he didn't seem particularly impressed by the Russian.

"The comrade colonel has some questions for you regarding the escape of the South Vietnamese colonel named Phuong," the military policeman explained. "He does not speak our language, but he does speak French. I believe you do too."

"Oui, Camarade Major," Lieutenant Ahn said.

Sogolov continued to peruse the documents in front of him. They told, in detail, of the escape of South Vietnamese Army Colonel Phuong Bai. The prisoner, while being transferred, managed to disarm his guard and kill that man as well as the driver of the car he was in. He left the bodies where they fell, and disappeared into the jungle. Phuong did not emerge again until communist agents noted his presence in Saigon only a month or so later. Sogolov raised his eyes and smiled at Lieutenant Ahn. *"Bon jour, Camarade Lieutenant."*

Ahn nodded back, his face blank.

"I am interested in the disappearance of Colonel Phuong Bai," Sogolov said. "It says here that you conducted the investigation of the incident. I believe this is your report, *non?"*

"Mais oui," Ahn said.

"May I ask, Lieutenant Ahn, where the prisoner was being taken?"

"To the military prison at Thai Nguyen, Comrade Colonel," Ahn answered.

"Pourquoi?"

"Because his interrogation in Hanoi had been completed," Ahn replied. "It is standard procedure. I have personally escorted many prisoners over there."

"I see, thank you," Sogolov said. He looked back at the report. "Who authorized the trip?"

"Je ne sais pas," Ahn answered with a shrug.

"Was it not the comrade General Truong Van?"

"I do not know," Ahn repeated.

"I believe the records state that Truong signed the transfer order personally," Sogolov pointed out.

"Really? I do not remember."

"I am also most curious about another thing," Sogolov said. "Why was the prisoner given a fresh set of clothing. I found this out by accident after interviewing the guards on duty in the cell block that night."

"I am not a member of the prison unit," Ahn said. "But I suppose the reason was to make him look more presentable if members of the public would see him."

"He was transferred at night," Sogolov pointed out. "No one could see that well inside a small command car."

"I am only supposing, Comrade Colonel," Ahn calmly said.

"Of course," Sogolov said agreeably. But inside, his mood seethed with anger. The clever Oriental officer was obviously evading the questions—even making fun of him. But there was no outward hostility from Ahn. Only that damned silent insolence. The KGB colonel went through the pretense of studying the report. "Were there any other officers involved in the transfer of the prisoner?"

"Do you mean as escorts?" Ahn asked.

Sogolov clenched his teeth in anger. *Of course not, you yellow-skinned weasel!* But he said, "No, Lieutenant. I mean in processing the paperwork or issuing the necessary orders."

"Only those going through their usual command and

staff procedures," Ahn answered.

"None instigated the action?"

"I don't know, Comrade Colonel."

"Yes. Thank you. I was wondering—" Sogolov paused for a couple of moments. "—was General Truong Van interested in the prisoner?"

"How do you mean?" Ahn asked.

"Did he interrogate Phuong? Or supervise the questioning?"

"I don't know, Comrade Colonel."

"Did you not interview him involving the escape?" Sogolov asked.

"No, Comrade Colonel," Ahn said. "If I had done so it would be in that report."

"Of course." Sogolov displayed a friendly smile. "By the way, did you know that Colonel Phuong Bai committed suicide in Saigon a few days ago?"

"No, Comrade Colonel."

"That hardly seems the act of a hero, does it?"

"No, Comrade Colonel."

"That is why I am wondering if someone did not help him escape for some reason," Sogolov said.

'A good deduction, Comrade Colonel."

"I think he had help and that someone had recruited him for a mission," Sogolov said.

"Really, Comrade Colonel?"

"Really, Comrade Lieutenant. I think there is something afoot that should be shared with the KGB," Sogolov said. "Anyone who is part of a cover-up will be in serious trouble."

"And rightfully so, Comrade Colonel!"

Sogolov again felt a surge of anger. "You are dismissed, Comrade Lieutenant."

"*Merci, Camarade Colonel. Bon jour.*" Ahn saluted and marched out of the room. He went outside the building and turned down the street toward the telephone exchange. Once there he shoved a few dong across the counter and went to one of the phone booths along the wall. He quickly dialed a number and waited.

"Huong here," came the answer.

"Comrade Colonel Huong," Ahn said. "This is Lieutenant Ahn. I have been examined by the KGB colonel called Sogolov."

"How did it go?" Colonel Huong asked.

"The Russian voiced his suspicion of the operation, Comrade Colonel," Ahn informed him. "I stuck to what I'd put in my official report."

There was laughter on the other end. *"Duoc roi!* When this mission is brought to a successful conclusion, that Russian bastard will have learned to respect the North Vietnamese intelligence service."

Ahn, smiling to himself, hung up.

Chapter 10

Captain Dan Reynolds of the 4041st Military Intelligence Detachment held on to his briefcase as he walked briskly down the hallway of the third floor in SOG's headquarters building. The military policeman who preceded him was a visual announcement that he had been cleared through all the security procedures, so none of the other MP guards challenged the captain or asked to check his ID and pass.

His escort stopped at an unmarked office and knocked.

Without waiting for a reply from within, the MP opened the door.

"Go ahead, sir."

"Thank you, Sergeant," Reynolds said. He stepped inside and immediately snapped to attention. "Captain Reynolds reporting as ordered, sir."

"Glad to see you, Captain," Brigadier General James Taggart replied. He indicated the man seated beside his desk. "I believe you know CIA Field Officer Charles Fagin."

"We're old friends," Reynolds said. "Hello, Chuck."

"How are you, Dan?" Fagin said.

"I believe you have a couple of dossiers to discuss with us," Taggart said. "Please take a seat and begin. We're a bit short on time."

"Yes, sir." Reynolds sat down and pulled out the first document from his briefcase. "Here we have the late

Colonel Phuong Bai of the South Vietnamese Army," Reynolds said.

Fagin smiled sardonically. "Who recently left the armed forces of his country via a self-inflicted bullet in the head."

"The same," Reynolds said. "He was actually a remarkable officer."

"Tell us about him," Taggart said stonily.

"Phuong came from one of South Vietnam's most wealthy families," Reynolds began. "In fact, they can trace their ancestry directly back to their country's ancient royalty."

Fagin chuckled. "So that was blue blood all over his desk, was it?"

"Indeed," Reynolds said. "They sent him to Paris for his education. The basic plan was for him to study economics and European business methods then join his father and older brothers in the family's commercial enterprise. That was a large export firm that had world-wide dealings."

Taggart lit a cigar. "I presume something got in the way of that plan, hey?"

"Yes, sir," Reynolds said. "Somehow the young man got some exposure to the military and was bitten by the soldiering bug. He begged his family to release him from their desires for a career in the export business and allow him to attend Saint Cyr."

"That's France's West Point," Fagin said. "I'd say he was going after becoming a professional soldier in a big way."

"Since he was the youngest son, there was no objection," Reynolds continued. "He completed his studies and received a commission as lieutenant of colonial infantry in 1938. He returned to French Indo-China—present day Vietnam—and was assigned to a line regiment."

"Ah!" Taggart exclaimed. "Then he wasn't always a staff officer."

"No, sir. When World War II broke out he fought against the Japanese. After France's armistice with Nazi Germany, he refused to cooperate with the Vichy government and joined a rebellious group of officers who conducted a deadly cat-and-mouse guerrilla warfare campaign against the occupying Japanese."

"That must have helped his career a lot," Fagin mused.

"It sure did," Reynolds agreed. "After Germany and Japan's ultimate defeat, he was well rewarded for his loyalty to France. When the war against the communist Viet Minh started, he was a battalion commander. Eventually, through a combination of opportunity and attrition, he was finally assigned to a staff position."

"Let me guess," Fagin said. "It wasn't an intelligence posting, was it?"

Reynolds grinned. "Give the man a cigar! It sure was. And it was his chance to show his natural brilliance in organizing and directing intelligence gathering against the enemy. A talent for sabotage also surfaced at this time while he went back to his old trade of unconventional warfare. He developed a very effective anti-guerrilla campaign against the Viet Minh. There were a couple of senior French officers who thought he was no less than a genius."

Fagin got up and went over to Taggart's bar to mix himself a drink. "So far you're telling us about a real clean-cut, dedicated, loyal professional officer. At this point I wouldn't be surprised if you told me the French didn't think his shit stank."

"That's a pretty close to their opinion of him," Reynolds said. "Naturally, after Dien Bien Phu fell and the two Vietnams were created, he continued on in his same job. But this time he was an officer in the new South

Vietnamese Army. He extended his area of operations up into the north."

"So how did he end up a prisoner?" Taggart wanted to know.

"Phuong wasn't satisfied with the results of some of his operatives," Reynolds explained. "He decided that the situation called for some 'hands-on' application on his part. He sneaked into the north and eventually got captured when things went from bad to worse."

"How long did they have him?" Fagin asked.

"We think close to a year," Reynolds said. "It is impossible to determine the exact date of his being compromised. At any rate, he eventually not only managed to escape, but came out with an announcement that he'd arranged for the defection of General Truong Van of the North Vietnamese intelligence service."

"Then he killed himself," Taggart said.

"Yes, sir," Reynolds said.

"Maybe Phuong wasn't the hero he was supposed to be," Fagin said. "I've been thinking long and hard on this. If a full blown commie general wants to defect, he knows that a special unit will be sent to pick him up. In Truong's case, his special knowledge would tell him that Falconi and his Black Eagles would be detailed to the mission."

"What are you getting at, Fagin?" Taggart asked.

"Phuong may have broken under interrogation," Fagin said. "This would give Truong the opportunity to either blackmail him into doing what he wanted, or fixing it up so the guy's disgrace would be hidden and he would be looked on as a hero. With Phuong considered completely trustworthy, we wouldn't hesitate to send Falconi out to get someone he'd reported ready to defect."

"I have a strong inclination to agree with you," Taggart said. He was thoughtful for several moments. "But

100

I'm not sure. Your theory is too pat, too logical. Intelligence matters are as diverse and illogical as camouflage patterns."

"Right now, I don't know how I'd bet," Fagin said bringing out his own uncertainty. He gestured to Reynolds. "What have you got on General Truong Van?"

"Not a hell of a lot," Reynolds admitted. "As far as we're concerned he didn't 'come into being' until only about five years ago. We know he is a highly-placed intelligence officer. That means he was probably trained in Moscow by the Russians."

"What's he been doing lately?" Taggart inquired.

"He's evidently a gifted linguist, and he's been acting as the senior liaison officer between the North Vietnamese Army and the Soviet KGB in his country."

"Was he associated with Colonel Gregori Krashchenko?" Fagin asked.

"Yeah," Reynolds said. "We think he may have even had something to do with the creation of the Red Bears."

"You mean that outfit that challenged the Black Eagles?" Taggart asked.

"Yes, sir. Six month ago, Truong was promoted to major general," Reynolds said.

Taggart ground out his cigar butt in the ashtray on his desk. "Now why would a son of a bitch like that decide to defect?"

"It's an open secret that my agency will pay plenty of money to a defecting general," Fagin said. "Hell, we'll set him up with a private income and put him in a big house just about any place in the free world he would like. All the information the guy would have would make it worth it."

"Hell, yes!" Reynolds agreed. "He could point out agents, safe houses, our own traitors, double-agents—the whole goddamned works!"

"Maybe the guy is a homosexual," Taggart said. He pointed to the dossier in Reynolds's hands. "Is there anything in there about his sexual preferences?"

"No, sir," Reynolds said.

"Now we have two possibilities," Taggart said. "He could be after money or about to get his taste for boys exposed. Perhaps even a combination of the two."

"There's always a chance he's had a change in ideology," Reynolds said. "It wouldn't be the first time."

"I don't know," Fagin said doubtfully. "He has a brilliant career going. I've got to come right out and say I think the guy is a phony."

"How are Falconi and his guys?" Reynolds asked. "All we know at MI is that they're out on an operation."

"They've disappeared," Fagin said. "We don't have the slightest clue where they might be."

"That's some real bad shit," Reynolds said, using an old army expression.

"Well, Captain, what's your opinion?" Taggart asked.

"I'm not sure," Reynolds said. "But the fact remains—the Black Eagle mission is obviously in serious jeopardy."

"Listen, General," Fagin said looking straight into Taggart's face. "I want permission to take that submarine and prowl the coast looking for those guys. What do you say?"

"The sub is still assigned to us," Taggart said. "Why not use it? Sure, Fagin. Go ahead. I'll get the paperwork rolling right away."

"Thanks, General Taggart," Fagin said.

"You'll need a lot of luck, Fagin," Taggart pointed out to him.

"I'll find 'em," Fagin said with a note of dogged determination in his voice.

"Even if you bring them back in body bags, it will

still take the generous smile of Dame Fortune to make that possible," Taggart said.

"That particular bitch hates me," Fagin said, going to the door. He turned and looked at the two other men. "So maybe I won't make it out of there either."

Lieutenant Anh was impatient. He grabbed the earphones off the head of the radio operator so hard that the man's ears turned red. The officer pressed them to his own. After listening a few moments, he flung them down and turned to glare furiously at the sergeant who was in charge of the communications room.

"Your equipment is faulty, Comrade Sergeant!"

The non-commissioned officer shook his head. *"Xin loi ong,* Comrade Lieutenant. But we have just performed our monthly maintenance check. Everything is in order and working perfectly."

Anh, without further comment, walked out of the building to the automobile waiting outside. He got into the back seat to join the other officer there. "The directional gear shows the signal growing weaker."

Colonel Huong shook his head. "That cannot be! Everything was checked out very carefully before the comrade general took the equipment into his possession."

"I listened myself, Comrade Colonel," Anh said. "The broadcasts are definitely losing strength."

"Bad luck!" Colonel Huong said. He leaned forward and tapped the driver on the shoulder. "Take us back to Hanoi."

Anh, sullen, stared out the window of the car. "If the battery-powered device dies off, Comrade General Truong will truly end up in enemy hands."

Huong nodded. "If that happens, the KGB will make sure that a few people get shot over the situation."

"Yes," Anh agreed. "North Vietnamese people."

"Not people," Huong disagreed. "Officers."

"At least the two patrol boats eliminated the submarine," Anh said hopefully. "The Black Eagles will be forced to move overland."

"*Co*," Huong agreed. "I will immediately dispatch several mobile teams to range down the possible escape routes to the south."

Anh's mood brightened a bit. "We shouldn't fret, Comrade Colonel. One way or the other, Falconi and his gangsters are locked in. It is only a matter of time until we discover their location."

Chapter 11

General Truong Van followed Blue Richards at a discreet distance. The American Navy Seal was clearing a path with wide swings of his machete. The general didn't want any of his own body parts to join the flying branches that were being chopped out of the way.

Blue finally stopped. He looked back at the NVA officer and showed a lazy grin. "Here it is, Gen'ral. You can bed down here for the day. The boys is gonna be spread out all around, so don't you fret 'bout nothin', heah?"

Truong, who spoke English, was never sure what the Alabamian was saying to him. The course at the University of Moscow had not covered any in-depth study of the Monroe County lingo. The general simply nodded his head. "Thank you very much."

"Yo're sure welcome," Blue said going out to his own position on the perimeter.

Truong used his boot to clear a spot under the shade of a palm tree whose huge fronds promised shelter from the sun. He crawled under the natural cover and settled in as best he could. After listening to make sure no one was around, he checked out the inside seam of his left jacket sleeve.

His hand found the small box. After a bit of feeling around, he located the on-off switch. A slight pressure of his thumb and the radio directional transmitter was turned off. There was no sense in wasting the energy cell.

The RDT was an East German transistorized instrument designed for tracking. It could be used by individuals, like Truong in this case, who wished to let someone know his location at all times. Or it could be hidden in a vehicle, or a person's clothing in order to do some fast and accurate tracking. Either way, it was a powerful little device that had a long range. The receiver designed for it was capable of pinpointing its exact location.

"General?"

Truong looked through the bushes and saw the Marine sergeant who was his escort approaching. "Over here, Comrade—er, excuse me—Sergeant Garcia."

"Some habits are hard to break, huh?" Paulo said.

"I suppose," Truong said. "You have been such a constant companion that I am beginning to think of you as a comrade."

"But not in the political sense, right?" Paulo asked with a grin.

"Of course not," Truong said.

"I'm settling in about ten meters over there," Paulo said. "Give a whistle if you need anything."

"I am fine. Thank you," Truong said. He watched the Marine walk away. Then he could hear some slight rustling as the man fixed up his resting place.

Then all was silent in the jungle.

Truong's mind turned over his predicament. He couldn't help but admire Falconi's bold decision not to do the obvious thing. No one would ever think the American commander would head to the north and actually use Red China as part of an escape route. But it made things perilous for him. If Falconi got the whole bunch down south, then Truong would be in one hell of a fix.

Any slipups on his part would result in a very unpleasant captivity. If he cooperated, he was assured the good life, but the last thing the general wanted was to betray his country. His love for Vietnam went far past politics or the dictates of the Soviet Union.

Finally, fretful and angry, he drifted off to sleep with the hope that Colonel Huong and Lieutenant Anh would finally figure out he and the Black Eagles were moving north and not south.

Truong Van had been born in a small farming village near the junctions of the Lo and Gam Rivers in north French Indo-China. His birth in 1925 added one more son to the five others his parents already had.

As a youngster, he was intelligent and sensitive to his surroundings. The village schoolmaster who taught Truong for the five years of education he received, felt that the lad was the one bright spot in a rather dull, almost useless, job. Most of the students were peasants born and bred, but Truong not only was a quick learner, but he was able to deal with the abstracts of political and philosophical thought. He turned into a voracious reader. The teacher was only too happy to see that the boy was supplied with good books to enjoy.

Contrary to what might be expected, Truong also liked the life of a rice farmer. The simple, hard labor he performed all day in the company of the other villagers seemed a pleasing contrast to quiet evenings of solitary reading. As he reached his teen years, Truong was popular among his peers and respected by the elders. But this happy attitude was not to last into his manhood.

Truong's native country was a French colony in those days. It was administered by France's civil service and military forces in a manner which exploited its natural products and the people's labor. Once a year the local magistrate dispatched his tax collectors out into the countryside to collect the monies due the colonial government from the natives. The tax rate was stiff and unrealistic. After the back-breaking stoop labor performed in a muddy rice paddy, Truong was loathe to part with any of his hard-earned money. He was particularly unhappy about it when he had to turn it over to a bearded, arrogant, demanding fat son of a bitch of a French bureaucrat who acted as if each separate franc had been his all along. Having learned French through the extra curricular activities of his teacher, Truong was able to express his displeasure directly to the Frenchman's face on a pleasant fall day in 1947 shortly after the Japanese had been driven from Indo-China.

The village farmers were standing in a long line before the Frenchman and his escort of colonial gendarmes. Each man reported in with his name. After checking a list, the tax collector stated how much the rice farmer owed. The man paid, then stepped away to let his neighbor perform his patriotic duty. When it was Truong's turn, he was already in a bad mood from standing out in the hot sun.

"Toi ten la Truong," he said presenting himself.

The bureaucrat looked down his list. Although he couldn't speak the people's language, he knew all the numbers. *"Nam tram* francs," he said.

Truong replied in French. *"C'est tres beaucoup*—it is too much."

"Eh?" the Frenchman asked astounded. "What is that you say?"

"You ask too much of me," Truong said. "It is nearly half my annual income."

"Alons! You speak French, hey?" the tax collector said. "Very impressive. I am sure you, as an educated man, earn more money than your ignorant fellow villagers. Therefore your taxes are six hundred rather than five hundred."

Truong came unglued at this point. He pointed his

finger in the Frenchman's face and yelled in rage at him. All this earned him was an extra fifty francs in taxes and a good ass-kicking by two of the gendarmes.

This experience taught more than the value of keeping one's mouth shut to the young man. He also learned to hate Europeans. White people, whether from France, Britain, Australia, or America, were European as far as he was concerned, particularly when they were in his country acting in an insulting and bullying manner.

Truong went back to his rice paddy after that. He grew sullen and resentful, even going so far as to accuse his neighbors of toadying up to the French. For awhile it seemed as if his angry voice was no more than a small bird's fart in the wind. Then a group of Vietnamese suddenly appeared in the village. They were armed and tough-looking.

At first the people were afraid they were bandits, but the visitors identified themselves as guerrilla soldiers of the Viet Minh—an organization formed for the sole purpose of kicking the French out of the country and reclaiming it for the indigenous population. They called everyone together and gave a long speech extolling their goals and politics.

Truong didn't give a damn about politics, but he liked the idea of running off the French. When the Viet Minh asked for volunteers to serve in their fighting army, the first to step forward was young Truong Van.

After going off to a training camp, he was assigned to a battalion that spent its time pulling ambushes on French army convoys along Colonial Route 1. Now, instead of having to line up in front of the colonists and fork over his money, Truong blasted them from camouflaged hiding positions with the PPSh41 submachine gun issued to him. He was an enthusiastic and spirited combat soldier.

Truong soon attracted favorable attention from his seniors and made some rank. Finally, after a solid year of serving as a section leader, he was sent up for an examination to see if he could possibly qualify for a commission as an officer. The man who interviewed him was a Moscow-trained, dedicated communist. After talking with the young fighter, this man decided Truong was qualified for greater things. A general education and IQ test was administered. Truong scored so high that he was immediately pulled out of the line, and arrangements were made to send him to the Soviet Union for a more thorough education.

Truong spent eight years in Russia. He attended various university classes, military academy courses, and specialist training. He learned foreign languages, military tactics and staff procedures, and was given a basic college-level political science education. He returned to French Indo-China in time to be assigned to General Giap's forces as a regimental intelligence officer at the Battle of Dien Bien Phu.

When his dream of seeing the French leave Vietnam was finally realized, Truong wanted to return to his home village. But pressure was put on him until he accepted an assignment as liaison officer between the North Vietnam Army and the Russian KGB in Hanoi.

He spent the next couple of years working with Lieutenant Colonel Gregori Kraschchenko. The Russian waged an impotent and futile campaign against a particular American officer and his unit—Falconi and the Black Eagles. The Russian finally formed his own elite unit and went out to take on Falconi eyeball-to-eyeball in a series of battles that were some of the fiercest and bloodiest of the entire Vietnamese War. But Kraschchenko was killed and his detachment of troops wiped out.

During all this time, Truong realized he hated Russians as much as he hated the French. They were just another oppressive minority in Vietnam as far as he was concerned. He was glad when Kraschchenko finally bought the farm. Truong made general, but a couple of weeks later he was saddled with another Russian. This time it was KGB Colonel Dimitri Sogolov.

Truong met a couple of other North Vietnamese officers who felt the same as he did. The end result of this rapport was that he, Colonel Huong, and Lieutenant Anh worked out a plan of their own to get the Black Eagles. By using the South Vietnamese colonel they'd broken during interrogation, the three could sucker the Americans into sending their most elite team of fighters if someone as important as a general of military intelligence wanted to defect. A physical meeting with the Black Eagles would give Truong the ability to lead the other two officers and a detachment of North Vietnamese troops straight to the American and his unit. The Radio Directional Transmitter would give his exact location at all times.

The patrol boats were brought into the scheme to keep the operation off the high seas. But rather than turn south as expected, the crafty Falconi had moved in the opposite direction—straight to Red China!

Now, with the RDT turned off, Truong napped under a bush in the jungle. Because of those former times of high-handedness by the French and Russians, the general was deadly determined that the plan would be successful.

Truong had slipped into a deep, restful sleep. It was like those wonderful naps in his boyhood when he went fishing on the river after the rice was harvested. With no hard work in the near future, it had been nice to be lazy in the warm weather and lie on the banks of the Gam

River waiting for his net to fill with large, delicious *ca* fish.

The general's slumber was interrupted by a rough pressure on his shoulder. He felt it again, then came awake. He looked over to see an American jungle boot nudging him. Truong looked up into the face of Marine Staff Sergeant Paulo Garcia.

Paulo smiled. "Nappy time is over, General"

"Ah!" Truong said. "We are resuming our journey?"

"Yes, sir," Paulo said respectfully.

Truong crawled out from under the bush and stood up. "Is Colonel Falconi still planning to take us into Red China?"

Paulo pointed. "Do you know what direction that is?"

"Of course," Truong answered. "It is north."

"Well, that's exactly the route the old man wants us to follow."

"He is a bold leader," Truong said, slipping on his pistol belt. He put his hand under the holster and bounced it a couple of times. "My weapon seems lighter somehow."

"Really?" Paulo said.

Truong smiled. "I am aware you removed my Tokarev and unloaded it, Sergeant Garcia."

"I guess I ain't as clever as I thought," Paulo said.

"Perhaps, I am *more* clever than you thought," Truong suggested. "Shall I lead the way back to the column?"

"Be my guest," Paulo invited.

As they moved toward the rest of the detachment, Truong casually slipped his hand up the sleeve of his jacket and turned on the Radio Directional Transmitter. He felt much better after the hours of sleep he had enjoyed. He was also more confident about the radio packet secreted in his uniform. By conserving the energy cell, the device could last for weeks.

Plenty of time to bring down his men on the Black Eagles.

Chapter 12

Chuck Fagin squeezed through the conning tower hatch, then slid down the ladder to the control room. When his feet hit the deck, he smiled at the submariners standing there. "Hi, guys. Long time no see."

"Nice to see you again, Mister Fagin."

Fagin turned to the sub's skipper. "Say, Mac, did you guys go through some overhaul and make those hatches smaller?"

"I'm afraid not, Chuck," Commander Lucas MacIntyre said, winking at him.

Fagin patted his belly. "Then it's a good thing I've got this chance to get out from behind my desk, huh? Maybe it'll be easier for me to get out of this boat than into it."

"I'd say so," MacIntyre said. "Get your gear and I'll take you back to your berth."

Fagin picked up his duffel bag that he'd already thrown through the hatch. He followed the skipper down to the area known as officers' country. The passageway was narrow, and the CIA man had trouble getting himself and bag down through it without bumping into the bulkheads. He was ushered into a small space that had a sliding curtain as a door. Inside was a small bunk, a folding desk, and a chair. A cupboard of sorts was to be used as a clothes closet. "So this is home, huh?"

"Be it ever so humble," MacIntyre added.

Fagin opened the top of the duffel bag and pulled out a shirt. "I'm glad you got hangers," he remarked.

"All for you, MacIntyre said. "Courtesy of the United States Navy."

"Now I'm sorry for all the nasty remarks I've made about our seaborne forces," Fagin said with a wink.

"You were referring to the surface craft navy, of course," MacIntyre said.

"Of course," Fagin said grinning. He began hanging up his clothes, his expression growing serious. "I've read all the official reports, Mac. But let me hear your version of what happened that night."

"Sure, Chuck," MacIntyre said. "We showed up at the exfiltration point right on time. In fact, when my radioman turned on his gear, he caught Falconi in the middle of a transmission."

"Was he using the proper call signs?" Fagin asked.

"He sure was."

"What about the code words to let you know everything was on the up and up?"

"He broadcast those too," MacIntyre said.

"Then everything must have been okay," Fagin said. "Falconi would never have risked you or your boat if there'd been any risk."

"I know Robert Falconi," MacIntyre said as a testimony to the army officer's personal courage and integrity.

"Okay. Then what happened."

"We came up to periscope depth and I made a check," MacIntyre said. "There was nothing to be seen on the horizon."

"A visual check, huh? What about radar? Were you employing any?"

"No way. Not this close and with Falconi giving us the go ahead," MacIntyre said. "Radar could give us away to ground stations, other seagoing craft, airplanes—"

"I get the picture," Fagin said. "So you surfaced."

"We started to," MacIntyre explained. "The conning tower broke clear. My exec and the reception party were ready to go up, then the North Vietnamese patrol boats appeared. There wasn't a goddamned thing we could do. Not one solitary goddamned thing!"

"Understandable," Fagin said. "Your orders were to haul ass in such a situation, right?"

"I hated those orders, Chuck."

"I know, Mac."

"We went back down, but came up for a quick periscope check," MacIntyre said. "All I saw were the enemy boats and the Black Eagle raft. It was empty."

"Shit," Fagin said. "We don't even know if Falconi and the guys made it."

"Right," MacIntyre said. "We tried radio contact, but we couldn't raise them."

"Falconi could have been too goddamned busy at that point to tend to commo," Fagin suggested.

"At that point, we had to go." MacIntyre lit a cigarette. "So what do you have in mind?"

"I'd like to go back to the rendezvous point," Fagin said. "Then let's cruise south and try to make radio contact. Maybe Falconi will be close enough to the coast to pick up our transmissions. Once he does, we can pick him up."

The sub skipper leaned against the bulkhead. "I'm all for this attempt, Chuck. So don't misunderstand my question. What do you think of our chances of finding Falconi?"

"You know that proverbial snowball in hell?"

"Yeah," MacIntyre said.

"About half that good," Fagin said.

116

Anh sipped his hot cup of tea. "Most puzzling, Comrade Colonel."

Sitting across from him in his Hanoi office in the NVA General Staff building, Colonel Huong agreed. "We must think carefully about this."

"Then let us analyze the situation," Anh said. "The comrade general's transmissions are growing weaker. And they are also turning off completely during the day. Yet every evening at the same time, they come back on the air."

"Comrade General Truong is a highly intelligent and crafty man," Colonel Huong said. "He is obviously turning the small set off and on purposely. I am sure there is a good reason for such enigmatic conduct on his part."

"I can only think that the Radio Directional Transmitter is faulty," Anh said. "It must be malfunctioning so badly that the general is nursing it along. Why else would he be conserving the energy cell?"

"Perhaps that isn't the problem at all," Colonel Huong mused. "Could it be that the American gangsters are watching him so closely that he cannot operate the device?"

"I think not, Comrade Colonel," Anh said. "There is no way they can know he has it unless they have a receiver tuned in on the exact frequency."

"If one of them grabbed the comrade general's arm, he might feel it," Huong said.

"That, too, is doubtful," Anh remarked. "I am strongly of the opinion that the comrade general is acting as he is in order to prolong the life of the energy cell."

"Of course," Huong agreed. "But he would only do such a thing because he feels there will be a delay in

117

the mission. But why?"

"Are they moving slowly?" Anh asked.

"I think not. But we don't know for sure. The weak signals give us no clues."

Anh thought a moment. "Perhaps they are not moving."

"If they are not moving, why is the signal growing weaker?" Huong asked. He shoved his tea cup forward.

Anh filled it from the pitcher at his elbow. "It is all most puzzling, Comrade Colonel."

Huong tasted the hot brew. "Indeed!"

"The aspect of the situation that bothers me is that damned signal," Anh mused. "No matter where we hear it from, it continues to grow weaker—weaker—" He stopped talking as his mind suddenly slipped into high gear. "Wait!"

"What, Comrade Lieutenant?" Huong asked.

"Comrade Colonel!" Anh shouted standing up. "The signal is lessening because the comrade general is not moving in the expected direction!"

"What are you talking about, Comrade Lieutenant?" Huong demanded to know.

"He is not moving to the south," Anh said. "He is moving to the north!"

"Call the communications center and have them switch their receiver antenna," Huong ordered.

"*Mau len*, Comrade Colonel." Anh got up from his chair and rushed to the telephone. He quickly dialed a number and got the military operator. "Give me the communications complex at Nam Dinh. Quickly!" He waited a few moments then had to go through the agonizingly slow process of getting the sergeant he wanted to talk to. When he finally reached the man, Anh wasted no time. "Go to the Radio Directional Receiver and turn it toward the north, Comrade Ser-

118

geant—don't ask questions—do as I say—turn it *bac!*"

Now Colonel Huong forgot his tea. He waited, nervously tapping his fingers against the table top.

Finally Anh spoke again. "Yes? Normal? *Duoc roi!* Now you know where to aim the equipment. Stay at your post, Comrade Sergeant! We will join you shortly!" Anh hung up. "They are moving north, Comrade Colonel!"

"You mean into Red China?" The colonel was thoughtful for a few moments. "How clever of Falconi."

"Not clever enough, Comrade Colonel," Anh said. "We are now able to draw the net shut and capture Falconi and his gangsters at last!"

General Hong Kim's official title was Chief of Staff of Military Intelligence of the People's Army of the Socialist Republic of North Vietnam. His position gave him awesome powers not only over other officers of the armed forces, but over the civilian population as well. A scrawled signature of his name was all it took to ruin a career, transfer an uncooperative character, throw somebody in prison, or even have someone executed without any due process of law or court-martial procedure.

Hong was feared and respected. Even higher-ups in the communist nation's inner-circles of government went out of their way to make sure they did not offend the gray-haired little man. He was coddled and pampered, complimented and patronized openly by those who wished to avoid the unpleasant consequences of crossing him.

But now the great general himself trembled with fear. He stood in the office of General Kuznetz in the

Russian Embassy. Kuznetz was the senior KGB officer in Southeast Asia. His own power, with the backing of the Kremlin, made Hong look like a minor Chinese warlord. And the angry expression on his face showed that he had every intention of unleashing his anger on the hapless North Vietnamese officer.

To make matter worse for Hong, there was another Russian KGB man in the same room also frowning at him. This was Colonel Dimitri Sogolov, the second-ranking man from that death-dealing Soviet organization.

"Who was in on Truong Van's disappearance?" Sogolov bellowed.

"I knew nothing of his disappearance, Comrade Colonel," Hong said. "He had signed out of the Hanoi military police headquarters to go to the Army Rest Center at Ha Coi. I thought he was still there until you informed me otherwise."

"Don't lie to me!" Sogolov yelled. "You knew all about it and I'm going to see that you come clean."

"Please, Comrade Colonel!" Hong begged.

General Kuznetz was calmer. "Comrade General Hong, all we ask is that you tell us what you know. I, personally, do not think you helped Truong flee. But I am strongly suspicious that you were covering it all up."

"Not at all, Comrade General," Hong said. "You must believe me. I am a good servant of the state and a brother to the Soviet Union."

Sogolov was unconvinced. "I do not believe that for moment. There is a conspiracy afoot here. It begins with the escape of the South Vietnamese colonel and grows more twisted and devious until we reach the point where Truong climbed over the wall behind his bungalow to disappear into the jungle."

"I am as shocked and outraged as you," Hong insisted.

"Lies! Lies!" Sogolov shouted. "The entire intelligence bureau of the North Vietnamese army is behind this."

"Not at all, Comrade Colonel," Hong said.

Kuznetz, still maintaining his cool, lit a cigarette. "I am beginning to think that way also, Comrade General Hong. You don't know how it galls me to even consider the possibility that you and your officers would turn against us. That you would hide facts from us and even aid one of your own generals in what even appears to be a defection."

Hong began to feel a bit angry. "May I remind you of something, Comrade General? Several years ago, Truong was taken out my jurisdiction and assigned as a liaison officer to work with the KGB in Vietnam. That action was instigated at your own personal insistence."

Now Kuznetz lost his cool. "Don't cloud the issue!"

Sogolov stepped into the picture. "That still would not stop a plot among you North Vietnamese intelligence officers, would it?"

Hong now appreciated the real seriousness of the situation. Neither Kuznetz nor Sogolov would become defensive when he pointed out that Truong was not even assigned to his command. The pair of Russians were going to hang somebody for what showed every evidence of becoming an embarrassing situation for themselves.

Hong decided to play the game too.

"Comrades, my men are well-trained and fully capable of carrying on a successful investigation into this matter," Hong said. "I promise you that within forty-eight hours I will be standing here with someone who can fill us all in on this most baffling case."

Kuznetz's expression was cold. "See that you do, Comrade General."

Hong, smiling weakly, saluted. He turned and hurried out of the room.

Chapter 13

The Black Eagle Detachment had been moving for almost two full hours, but their progress had been damnably slow. Archie Dobbs, as the scout, had to constantly call halts while he went forward to investigate activities ahead on the route he had chosen. There seemed to be a whole series of disturbances that were broken up by intermittent periods of deadly silence.

Even the flankers were coming in with alarming reports on signs of increased North Vietnamese troop activity. There were fresh trails, footprints, and small abandoned campsites where patrols had stopped for a meal and rest.

Archie, after a dozen stops and starts, finally returned to the column and sought out Lieutenant Colonel Robert Falconi.

"Sir, the map doesn't show any military sites in this area, but the place is crawling with NVA troops," Archie complained. "It's almost like there's a large garrison nearby.

Falconi was also perturbed. "We're almost right on top of the Chinese border," he said. "I don't understand why the North Vietnamese would have such heavy concentrations of units around here."

Archie was thoughtful for a couple of moments.

"Do you suppose they're having maneuvers of some kind? Maybe we stumbled into the middle of an FTX."

"A Field Training Exercise?" Falconi mused. "I don't know about that. I can't recall seeing any intelligence data on maneuver areas this far north."

Ray Swift Elk, standing nearby, offered a good suggestion. "Hell, sir, we've got a goddamned bona fide North Vietnamese general with us. Let's ask him."

Falconi laughed. "Sometimes the obvious really escapes you, doesn't it. Okay, Archie. Go fetch him up here."

"Yes, sir." Archie walked back down the column. He hardly ever saw the guys any more it seemed. He was always up to the front out of sight, only coming back to talk to Falconi. As he passed them, he grinned to each, sometimes giving one a friendly pat on the shoulder. He finally reached Paulo and General Truong.

"Hey, Arch," Paulo said. "What brings you back here to the slums."

"Colonel Falconi wants to talk with the general here," Archie said. "C'mon."

"Of course," Truong said. He followed Archie back up to Falconi with Paulo trailing after them.

Falconi nodded a friendly greeting to the North Vietnamese general. "How are you?"

"Tolerable, thank you," Truong replied. "Sergeant Garcia is an agreeable companion."

"We've been noticing an increase in NVA troop activity in the area, General," Falconi said. "Perhaps you could explain that to us."

"Of course, Colonel," Truong replied. "There have been numerous clashes between North Vietnamese soldiers and those of Red China in this area. My government has been forced to maintain a strong concentration of frontline units here."

Falconi was puzzled. "Do you mean to tell me that two communist nations have been shooting at each other?"

Truong smiled. "You realize, of course, that both countries have not allowed any publicity on the incidents. If you studied the history of this land, you will find that the Vietnamese and Chinese are ancient enemies."

"Jesus!" Archie exclaimed. "I knew the Rooskies and the Chinese were going at each other's throats, but I didn't know nothing about the North Vietnamese getting in on it."

Truong continued. "There have been numerous excursions into each other's territory and even some artillery duels. The hostilities have grown worse in the last year or so."

"The situation sounds damned serious," Falconi said.

"I fear that it is," Truong said. "At this moment we are in a war zone as active as what is going on between the NVA, Viet Cong and your side. I would like to make a strong suggestion if you don't mind, Colonel Falconi. My E&E net lies to the south. I must point out that we would be much safer if we pulled back and utilized that facility. I personally guarantee its effectiveness."

Falconi shook his head. "Archie, continue the march. Just stay extra alert and don't lead us into any bad situations."

"I'll do my best, sir," Archie promised.

"What you ask of this brave soldier is impossible," Truong said. "We cannot help but blunder into sol-

125

diers—either North Vietnamese or Chinese."

Archie grinned. "What's that favorite saying of yours, Colonel Falconi?"

"You mean the one that goes, 'Nobody said this job was going to be easy'?" Falconi answered.

"That's the one, sir," Archie said stepping out. "Follow me, guys."

Archie moved ahead. He employed the "Georgia High-Step." This method of walking, utilized in the U.S. Army's Ranger School at Fort Benning, Georgia, consisted of slow deliberate steps. The foot was raised high, then gently set down while feeling for twigs, dry leaves or any other noise-producing debris before full weight was put on it. This made for slow travel, but it was silent and deadly.

Archie, every nerve, sense and instinct in his body on screaming alert, held his M16 rifle at high port. He, like the others in the detachment, had removed the sling so it would not get caught in bushes or limbs. The safety of the weapon was off and his finger rested on the trigger guard rather than directly on the trigger. That way, if he accidentally stumbled or fell, he would not inadvertently fire the weapon. Not only would such a mishap make noise, but he also might very well shoot himself in the bargain.

After a half hour, Archie grew extremely nervous. He came to a complete halt. He tried to peer through the dense jungle vegetation but could see nothing. He slowly turned his head as he strained his ears to hear any sort of warning sounds. Archie spent a full five minutes in this nervous activity. Finally, taking a deep breath, he started into one more Georgia High Step.

And the bark on a tree by his head exploded.

The sniper fired again, this time coming even

126

closer. Archie, not knowing where the bad guy was, went straight to the ground. He fired a couple of shots back to cover himself, then scrambled back toward the column.

Falconi heard the shots. He waved back at Blue and Malpractice behind him. "Move up and give Archie a hand."

"Aye, aye, sir!" Blue said.

The two Black Eagles scrambled forward. They had gone only a few meters when they bumped into Archie coming the other way. The scout was glad to see the reinforcements. "C'mon, guys. This way," he said turning around to lead them back.

They came under fire less than a minute later. But this time, Archie spotted the sniper. He was up in a tree, well situated on a platform of branches. Archie, not having time to carefully aim, slipped his selector on full automatic. He pointed upward and pulled the trigger. The fusillade blew branches, bark, leaves, and one North Vietnamese soldier out of the tree. The Red, already a corpse, hit the ground with a loud clump.

But he had friends nearby.

A skirmish line of NVA broke into view. They hosed AK47 fire toward the three Black Eagles. Falconi's men had no choice but to throw back a quick return volley, then haul ass out of the area.

They rushed through the brush and rejoined the detachment in time to find that Falconi had formed a firing line of his own. The only people not on it were Paulo and his personal charge, General Truong Van. They had pulled back to the rear, ready to go rearward or forward, whatever the fortunes of the growing battle dictated.

Archie, Blue and Malpractice were put into posi-

127

tion by Top Gordon. They settled in just in time. North Vietnamese troops, sweeping forward in platoon strength, charged the Black Eagle position.

Falconi's men, acting as an infantry squad with Gunnar Olson and Calvin Culpepper as automatic riflemen, blasted out in classic military defensive volleys. Each man had his area of fire that criss-crossed with the guys beside him.

The NVA, screaming in rage, swept forward. Their first rank crumpled to the ground under the Black Eagles' salvos of 5.56-millimeter bullets. Their buddies behind them pressed on, leaping over the bodies and charging ahead. But they, too, collapsed in the withering sprays of Black Eagle bullets.

The third line of North Vietnamese were slowed by the corpses in front of them. They stumbled through the carpet of their fallen comrades, then were pitched on top of the dead as the swarms of bullets slapped into their ranks.

The fourth and final row of enemy riflemen managed to get halfway through their dead. They hesitated a moment, then returned fire. A few of them were pitched to the ground under the bursts of incoming rounds from the Black Eagles. Finally their commander ordered a withdrawal. The remnants of the NVA platoon pulled back and disappeared deeper into the jungle.

"Okay, guys!" Falconi shouted. "Move forward. Take it easy and mind your fields of fire."

"And stay aligned goddamnit!" Top added with a bellow.

The detachment continued to advance for twenty meters without meeting any resistance. Suddenly, however, North Vietnamese fire broke out ahead.

"Hit the dirt!" Falconi yelled. "Return fire!"

The Black Eagles immediately responded. Several had to crawl forward to find good firing positions. Once settled in, they began an exchange of shooting with a nearly unseen enemy. The one comforting thought was that the NVA could not see them well either.

Falconi popped up a couple of times to deliver well-aimed automatic fire bursts in the direction of the Reds. He looked around for his sergeant major. "Top! Top!"

Top Gordon, hearing his name, left his position and crawled through the jungle to join the commander. "Yes, sir?"

"The NVA are not in a well-prepared position," Falconi said. "They simply stopped and turned at a convenient place in order to slow us down."

"I agree, sir," Top said. "Got any ideas?"

"Yeah," Falconi said. "I want you to take Gunnar and Archie. You guys make a feint attack on the left side of the North Vietnamese line. Once they engage you, pull back a bit and keep 'em occupied."

"I got you, sir."

"In the meantime, I'll take the rest of the detachment and go around on the other side and make a flanking attack. We should be able to roll 'em up."

"Yes, sir." Top scurried away to tend to his side of the battle.

Paulo Garcia and General Truong Van lay low in the back of the battle formation. They kept out of the way as they moved with the tide of fighting that swept through the jungle. Truong openly praised Falconi. "He is a natural jungle fighter," he said. "He maintains strict control in spite of poor visibility and conditions that make maneuver difficult."

"Yeah," Paulo agreed. "But he'd do damned good

129

in any combat situation. Hell, Colonel Falconi can fight in city, swamp, open country, mountains—you name it."

Truong only nodded. Now he really appreciated the hell that the KGB officer Gregori Krashchenko must have gone through when leading his Red Bears against the Black Eagles.

Top led Gunnar and Archie over to the left side of the fighting. Calvin Culpepper was the last man on that side of the line. The black trooper, called "Buffalo Soldier" by Ray Swift Elk, waved to them. "Hold 'em down, boys," he called out. "We'll roll 'em as quick as we can."

"Right on!" Archie called out.

When the three got into position at the far side of the battlefield, they spread out and moved forward. Once contact was made, they made no further attempts at advancing. The trio of Black Eagles settled in behind the best cover they could find and began to pour hot slugs into the enemy position.

By that time Falconi had gotten the other five men at the best place to launch a deadly flanking attack. When he gave the word, they swept forward in a yelling, blasting, streamrolling attack.

The NVA did the best they could. Their attention had been drawn to the opposite end of their formation by Top, Gunnar, and Archie. Now with the surprise assault coming in from the far side, they tried to stem it. NVA officers cursed and turned their sections, but there was little they could do. Drawn off balance and out of position, they offered little resistance. After the initial unlucky casualties were dumped to the ground in the salvos, the North Vietnamese were routed. Completely out of control, they broke and ran in scattered groups. The unit was no longer a military outfit.

It had been reduced to a few panic-stricken survivors.

When the jungle grew quiet, Top led Archie and Gunnar forward to link up with the rest of the detachment. They found the other six waiting for them amidst the sprawled corpses of NVA.

"Sir," Archie said grinning. "You're a goddamned tactical genius."

Falconi winked at him. "You guys inspire me."

Paulo and Truong now came up and joined the group. Truong, furious at the sight of his slaughtered countrymen, barely managed to control himself. He stood silently, avoiding a look at the dead NVA.

Falconi glanced at Paulo. "How's it going?"

"We're okay, sir," Paulo said. "It's a little nerve wracking not knowing for sure what's going on, though."

"Keep hanging back," Falconi said. "This battle isn't over yet." He turned to the men. "As skirmishers, let's move out. Those bastards might try it again."

Once again aligned in the classical infantry formation, the Black Eagles advanced through the jungle. They had to keep close to maintain contact and be able to offer the maximum of frontal fire power.

After a short ten minutes, they really needed it.

A thin but well-camouflaged group of NVA suddenly made themselves known by a coordinated fusillade into Falconi's detachment. The Black Eagles had no choice but to press forward. They picked up the pace and damned the luck as they blindly hosed the area in front of them with swarms of 5.56-millimeter bullets. Cries of shock and pain showed their fire was accurate. The resistance melted away and they moved through more scattered bodies.

"Slow it down, but keep aligned," Falconi cautioned them. "We can't go back. There's nothing there but the rest of the North Vietnamese Army." Suddenly he laughed. "Of course the entire Red Chinese Army is straight ahead."

"Thank you, sir," Archie said with a sardonic smile. "I really needed that."

He'd no sooner spoken than a sharp, short whistle sounded in the air. This was followed by a loud explosion behind them.

"Mortars!" someone yelled.

"Double-time! Double-time!" Falconi ordered. "They'll get our range."

Now the detachment went forward at a rapid trot. More mortar rounds detonated behind them, but the impacts of the shells was drawing closer.

"Faster!" Top urged them.

Now running, they crashed forward to avoid being blasted to bits. They broke through the tree line into a clearing. The mortar crew who had been firing at them was set up there. The North Vietnamese looked at the sudden appearance of the Americans with a mixture of shock and fear.

Nine M16 rifles emptied their magazines into the hapless mortarmen. The NVA died at their weapon, their bodies falling amidst the ammo boxes and the tube of the weapon.

Archie looked around at what was left of the mortar crew. "Those guys won't bother us no more, sir. But there's got to be others around."

"Yeah," Falconi agreed. "Especially with the NVA nervous about Chinese infiltration. We've got to put some distance between ourselves and this latest unpleasantness." He winked at the scout. "Do you think you can lead us out of here through the dark?"

"Sure," Archie said. "It might be difficult, but I

can manage it."

"Comparatively speaking, it will be easy," Falconi said. "The real problem comes tomorrow when we have to cross that Chinese border."

"Yeah," Archie said. "The shit is really going to hit the fan then."

Chapter 14

Chuck Fagin lay on his bunk staring up at the rivets in the steel overhead. He started to drift off to sleep again, but fought the fatigue until he could make his eyes stay open on their own accord. "God!" he moaned to himself. "I've got to get out of this bunk. I've just got to!"

Finally he sat up and swung his legs over the side. The deck was cold on his bare feet. He went to the cupboard-like closet and pulled out his clothing. The CIA man quickly dressed, then pulled the curtain aside and stepped out into the passageway.

The gallery was on the way to the radio room. He stopped by and gave a friendly nod to the mess cook on duty. "What's a guy have to do for a cup of coffee around here?"

"Just ask, Mister Fagin," the young submariner said pleasantly. He took a heavy mug and filled it with strong, hot coffee. "Can I interest you in some chow? I'd be happy to rustle up some bacon and eggs."

"That's real nice," Fagin said. "But no thanks. I don't eat breakfast, and I got a lot of commo work ahead of me."

"I hear you went thirty-six straight hours on radio watch," the cook said.

"Yeah," Fagin said taking a sip of the strong brew. "And it looks like I'll be doing it again."

"Maybe you'll make contact," the sailor said hopefully.

"Maybe. Thanks for the coffee."

"Anytime, Mister Fagin."

Fagin waved back over his shoulder as he walked away. He went down to the radio room. He leaned inside the small cubbyhole. "How's it going?"

The radioman, a veteran petty officer, looked up. "Pretty much the same, Mister Fagin. I'm afraid I don't have any good news. We haven't been able to pick up Falcon."

"How often have you been transmitting?" Fagin asked.

"Every fifteen minutes," the sailor said.

Fagin took a sip of the coffee. "Damn! Where the hell could Falconi and the guys have gotten off to?"

"Mister Fagin, I guess you know we all feel awful about leaving them there that night," the submariner said. "We'd've given anything to have waited."

"Nobody's holding anything against the *Perch*," Fagin said. "MacIntyre did exactly as he should have."

"The skipper's feeling rotten too," the radioman added.

"Yeah. I talked with him," Fagin said. "Say, you look like you could use a break."

"I sure could," the sailor said. "These earphones feel like they're pushing my ears into my skull."

"I'll take over if you want," Fagin offered. "Go get some coffee."

"Great!" The submariner slid out of the small space.

Fagin took his place. He handed him his cup.

135

"You wouldn't mind getting me a refill, would you? It's going to be a long, long day."

"I'd be glad to, Mister Fagin."

Fagin turned his attention to the radio. He picked up the microphone and hit the transmit button. "Falcon, this is Moby Dick. Over. Falcon, this is Moby Dick. Over."

The only sound over the earphones was ominous dead air.

"Shit!" he swore. Then he transmitted again. "Falcon, this is Moby Dick. Over. Falcon, this is Moby Dick. Over."

The reward for his effort was deadly silence.

The Chinese border guard post was well-manned and equipped. Archie Dobbs, studying the place through his binoculars, noted the sandbagged entrenchments, bunkers, and barbed wire. There was plenty of evidence that the North Vietnamese had landed some high explosive artillery shells in the area. Craters, split sandbags, and a couple of ruined structures gave grim testimony to the small unpublicized war going on in the vicinity.

Archie turned and signaled back at the rest of the detachment. His gestures indicated they were to go farther down toward the left. After they moved off, he pulled back from his observation post and hurried off to catch up with them.

When Archie joined the detachment ten minutes later, Falconi wanted all the information the scout had picked up on his reconnaissance.

"There's a border guard station up that way, sir,"

Archie reported. "It's well-fortified."

"Do you think we could take it with M16s?" Falconi asked.

Archie shook his head. "No, sir. I could tell they'd been pounded with plenty of artillery. A lot of it was tore up, but the bunker and entrenchments are standing tall. Them guys are ready for big stuff."

"Sounds like they'd just sit in there and pick us off one by one through their firing slits," Falconi mused.

"That's the name of that game, sir," Archie agreed.

"Did you find any good places to cross over into China?"

"Most of the border is covered by barbed-wire," Archie said. "It's prob'ly got sound detection devices hooked to it. If a bird pissed on it, them guys at the border post would know about it."

"Any open areas?" Falconi asked.

"Yes, sir. A wide one. And far out of sight of that station too," Archie said. "But you know what that means."

"I sure as hell do," Falconi said. "Mines."

"From the looks of the area, it's one big mine field," Archie said.

"Get me our resident demo experts," Falconi said.

"You mean *Monsieur* Blue Richards and *Monsieur* Calvin Culpepper?" Archie asked.

"Yeah. And tell those *messieurs* to shake their asses."

"Yes, sir!"

Archie rushed off and returned in less than a minute with Blue and Calvin dutifully following. "Here they are," he announced.

Calvin and Blue, with their M16s slung over their shoulders, stood easy in front of their commander. Calvin smiled. "We hear you need some demolition dudes, sir."

"That's right," Falconi said.

"Do you want us to blow somethin' up?" Blue asked.

"No. As a matter of fact, I want you to do the opposite. Your job is going to be preventing explosions," Falconi said. "There's a mine field we have to clear before we can cross it into China."

"I cain't recall seein' no fancy mine detection equipment the last time I looked into my patrol pack," Blue said. "So I reckon we'll have to use these." He reached down and whipped out his bayonet."

"That's all I've got too, sir," Calvin said.

"Do your best," Falconi said. "Let's go, Archie."

Archie turned with a gesture for everyone to follow him. The intrepid scout, with the entire detachment spread out behind him, took a roundabout way back through the jungle until he reached the spot where the suspected mine field lay. He pointed through the trees to an open field bordered by trees. "That's it, guys. Good luck."

"Cover us," Blue said grimly. "C'mon, Calvin, ol' buddy."

"Let's go," Calvin said.

The Black Eagles spread out in the cover of the heavy brush in order to take care of any interlopers that might unexpectedly arrive. Meanwhile, snaking forward on their bellies, Blue and Calvin went to work.

The two demo men worked several meters apart. They carefully slid their bayonet blades into the earth at a shallow angle. After making several slow penetrations, they would move ahead a bit, then try again. The pair went about the task methodically for twenty minutes before Blue's blade hit something solid.

"I got somethin', Calvin."

"Hang on. I'm coming over," Calvin said. He probed ahead of himself until he reached his companion. "Now let's see what somebody put down here for us."

They carefully worked their way around the buried object until its outline was finally obvious to them. Then they removed the dirt a bladeful at a time until they got their first glimpse of the thing.

"It's made outta wood," Blue said.

"Yeah. Typical Chinese manufacture," Calvin said. "Let's clear some more away from it." Another ten minutes went by before the mine was fully exposed.

Blue whistled. "That there, ol' buddy, is a Russian PMD-6," he said.

"I think it's a Chinese copy," Calvin said. "Look at the writing on it."

"Yeah. But it works the same."

The mine was 7.5 inches long, 3.5 inches high, and 2.5 inches long. No more than a wooden box with a firing device, the explosive inside was deadly TNT.

Blue studied it again. "Whoops! Look at that wire leading off from the trigger mechanism."

139

Calvin grimaced. "Those sonofabitches! It's hooked up to others. That means if one goes off, all go with it."

"We'd better check things out real good," Blue said.

"Okay," Calvin agreed.

The two resumed their bayonet search. Finally, a half hour later, they knew what they were facing.

"What we got here," Blue said. "Is anti-personnel mines arranged in a trip wire box-pattern."

"Yep," Calvin said. "One pull on the wire will set off four mines. Did you find any anti-tank or anti-vehicle stuff?"

"Nope. I reckon them Chinese is expectin' foot traffic in this area," Calvin said. He sighed. "Well, let's finish up here and clear a path through this dang meadow so the boys can cross over."

"Yeah. But let's not hurry," Calvin said. "One slip and we're both hamburger."

"Hell, ol' buddy! I didn't say I was all that anxious to see China."

Now they went to work with a purpose. They chose the shortest route across the field. Using the bayonet method, Blue and Calvin made sure there was a six-foot wide "trail" through the mines. It took two solid hours of non-stop work, but when they were finished, they stood inside Red China.

Falconi, studying them through his binoculars, saw them gesture it was all right to follow. He nudged Top. "Okay. Let's lead the guys across. Just make sure they stay single file and go in the exact route I take."

"You bet, sir."

140

Two minutes later, the seven Black Eagles walked slowly down the track opened by Blue and Calvin. When they reached the other side, they went quickly into the cover offered by the jungle.

"Let's give the guys a break, Sergeant Major," Falconi said. "They deserve it."

"Yes, sir," Top said. He looked around. "So this is China, huh? I remember when I was a kid reading about the old soldiers who served here. It kinda makes you stand in awe, don't it?"

"Not really," Falconi said. "Frankly, my mind is racing with trying to figure a way to get the hell out of this goddamned place."

The communications sergeant smiled. "The signals are now much stronger, Comrade Lieutenant."

Lieutenant Anh, bracing himself against the rocking of the patrol boat on the choppy waves, nodded his approval. "Do they show a continued movement to the north?"

"Yes, Comrade Lieutenant." The sergeant, a specialist in radio tracking equipment, had been brought aboard the boat along with his equipment. He continued to work the dial on the receiver. "The transmissions are coming from the vicinity of the Chinese border. However it is difficult at this time to pinpoint which side."

"Any further movement will clear that up," Anh said encouragingly. "Keep up the good work, Comrade Sergeant."

"*Cam on ong*, Comrade Lieutenant."

Anh looked at the navy helmsman guiding the

boat. "Make sure you pay strict attention to the comrade sergeant. It is important that we sail directly to the location of the radio broadcasts."

The helmsman nodded, alert for any directional changes requested by the army communications man.

Anh stepped off the flying bridge, going down the ladder to the small boat's cockpit deck. He glanced outward and could see the other two vessels that made up their small armada. These were the same craft used to break up the Black Eagles' submarine exfiltration. The largest patrol boat had a helicopter landing pad located aft. At that moment, an Mi-24 Hind gunship was lashed down on it.

Anh stepped into the main cabin where Colonel Huong waited. The lieutenant saluted. "The radio tracking operation is working well, Comrade Colonel."

"Excellent," Huong said. He shook his head. "I cannot figure why the gangster Falconi would do such a foolhardy thing as moving north into China. Was it not Comrade General Truong's plan to lure him and his men into a bogus escape-and-evasion net?"

"Yes, Comrade Colonel," Anh said. "Perhaps Falconi thought we would launch an extensive southerly search for him. He no doubt hoped we would not finally figure he was going the long way."

Huong laughed. "He underestimated our intelligence, didn't he, Comrade Lieutenant?"

"Exactly as the Russians are doing," Anh said.

"Yet I wonder about his entire escape plan," Huong said thoughtfully. "Could it be that the move north was part of a contingency? Perhaps the American submarine is part of that alternate scheme. There might even be aircraft involved in his bid for freedom."

Anh shrugged. "It does not matter, Comrade Colonel. We have these patrol boats equipped with sonar to deal with the submarine. Our third vessel boasts a helicopter gunship to deal with any troop carrying transport that the Americans might employ in an attempt to remove Falconi and the Black Eagles."

"You are correct, of course, Comrade Lieutenant," Huong said. "We are able to home in on the exact—the *exact*—location of the Americans and the comrade general. No matter what sort of escape they plan, we will be able to react accurately and in a timely manner."

"They cannot escape," Anh said. "There is no way."

Colonel Huong lit a cigarette. "It is only a matter of time, Comrade Lieutenant Anh. We have the entire area sewn up tight. No one can possibly get in and make contact with Falconi without our knowledge. And he cannot get out for the same reason."

The lieutenant agreed. "*Co*, Comrade Colonel! And I cannot wait to see the KGBs' faces when we display the Black Eagles to them. Whether as live prisoners or cadavers, the glory will be ours as North Vietnamese!"

Chapter 15

The guard saluted smartly, then turned and banged his fist on the heavy steel door. An Oriental face appeared in the small barred window of the portal. The red collar tabs on the man's green uniform showed that he, too, was a soldier. He displayed a frown. *"Co?"* he asked.

"The visitors for General Hong have arrived," the exterior guard said in a brisk manner.

"Mau len!" came back a respectful exclamation.

A heavy rattle of a large padlock being unlocked could be heard. This was followed by a rusty bolt being slid across a hinge. The heavy door squeaked horribly as it was laboriously pulled open.

The other sentry also exhibited a sharp salute. *"Moi ong vao,"* he said.

General Vladimir Kuznetz and Colonel Dimitri Sogolov stepped inside the entrance yard of the Hanoi District Military Prison. The two KGB officers were politely asked to wait while the guard cranked an old-fashioned telephone mounted on the wall by the same door he had just worked so hard in opening.

Within moments a young officer appeared. He spoke fluent Russian. "Good evening, Comrades," he said. "The comrade general awaits your pleasure in his office. Please be so kind as to follow me."

They were taken through yet another steel door. The three men walked across a stone courtyard bordered by cell blocks. Sogolov noticed a squad of riflemen standing in formation in one corner. He pointed to the soldiers. "Who are they, Comrade?" he asked.

The North Vietnamese officer looked back at him and smiled. "They are a firing squad, Comrade Colonel."

"There is to be an execution soon?" Sogolov asked.

"Yes," the NVA man said. He gestured to the Russians. "Please come with me up the stairs."

The trio went up to the second floor of the administration building. The officer rapped on a door, then opened it. "Please enter, Comrades."

The Russians stepped into the office. The room was spartan in appearance with only a floor lamp, and a large, scarred desk with two chairs sitting in front of it. General Hong Kim, the Chief of Staff of Intelligence for the North Vietnamese Army, sat in a third chair behind the desk. He stood up and smiled politely. "Good evening, Comrades."

"Good evening, Comrade General," Kuznetz said, thinking the man looked like the cat from the cliche who had just swallowed the canary. "It is very nice to see you again."

"Equally for me, let me assure you," Hong said. "Please to sit down, thank you." He pulled a bell from his desk drawer and tinkled it. "I will have coffee served."

"Thank you," Kuznetz said. He was in a hurry to get down to business, but he knew he had to put up with the Oriental custom of not launching immediately into any main topics. "You remember Colonel Sogolov, of course."

"Of course!" Hong said, delighted. "And it is a pleasure to see you, Comrade Colonel."

"Thank you, Comrade General," Sogolov said.

There was a light rapping on the door. A white-jacketed orderly appeared pushing a tea cart. He had evidently been well instructed. He went first to General Kuznetz and poured him a cup of coffee. After holding up a small wooden tray with rice cakes and shrimp rolls, he rolled his contraption over to Colonel Sogolov.

Hong seemed as pleased as a young girl holding her first party. "Please! Help yourselves. I beg your pardon for the lack of European food, but the bombing of Haiphong harbor by the imperialist gangsters has destroyed the latest shipments."

"Please don't apologize," Kuznetz said diplomatically. "These refreshments are delicious, really."

"Truly they are," Sogolov added.

Hong was served last. He slowly sipped his coffee and nibbled a rice cake while carrying on a near one-sided, tiresome conversation. The two Soviets endured the repast, trying to drop strong hints to hurry up by gulping their coffee. This only made the orderly step forward and refill their cups each time.

But finally Hong finished. The orderly methodically went about once more with his cart picking up the cups, saucers, and small plates. After affecting a

146

slight bow to the three officers, he withdrew and left them, shutting the door.

Kuznetz decided to lead things himself. "You cannot imagine our excitement when we received your message, Comrade General," he said.

"Ah, yes!" Hong said. "Did I not tell you that I would leave not one stone unturned in a relentless investigation."

"Yes, you did," Kuznetz said. "We had complete faith in your ability to get to the truth in the matter of Truong Van's disappearance." He turned to his companion. "Is that not so, Comrade Colonel Sogolov."

"Yes, indeed," Sogolov responded properly.

"I began by interrogating the comrade general's driver," Hong said. "He displayed such nervousness that I suspected he was guilty." He shrugged. "Of course it occurred to me that he was ill at ease because of my rank. Sometimes soldiers are like that, you know."

"Yes, yes," Kuznetz said impatiently. "It is the same in the Russian Army. Please go on."

"But his shifty eyes did not escape my observation, so I pressed on," Hong said.

Sogolov smirked inwardly. In his mind all Oriental eyes seemed shifty.

"The soldier began stammering after awhile, so I became more stern and spoke to him as a father would do to an erring son," Hong said. "Sometimes such tactics are better than brute force, Comrades."

"Yes! Yes! Please!" Kuznetz begged.

"Finally, he broke down into tears and begged forgiveness," Hong said. "The young man was utterly broken and ashamed for what he had done."

"What had he done actually?" Sogolov asked.

"I am getting to that," Hong answered. "He looked so boyish with the tears running down his face. He actually fell on his knees, Comrades. He grasped my hands and wept like a baby. 'There is only one thing you can do,' I told him. 'Confess all and throw yourself on the merciful justice of the people's government.' "

"And is that what he did?" Kuznetz asked.

"Of course," Hong said. "He told me that the comrade general had been acting suspiciously for months. He knew he should have reported, but didn't. 'A good communist never hesitates to turn in suspicious person,' I admonished him."

"Most commendable, Comrade General," Kuznetz said. "Would it be possible for us to talk to him?"

"I think not," Hong said with a smile. "I saw to it that he was transferred to the fighting in the south. Facing the danger and hardships of battle will cleanse his soul and conscience."

"It would seem you learned little from the soldier," Sogolov interjected in an irritated voice.

"Oh, I learned plenty," Hong assured him. "He gave me the name of an officer. Just one, solitary, single name." He lit a cigarette. "But that was all I needed."

"Of course," Kuznetz said. "No one doubts your professionalism, General Hong."

"I had the officer arrested and brought here to the

148

prison," Hong said. "Dealing with him was not the same as with the honest young soldier. The man, a major, was deceitful and crafty. He hid the truth in the jungle of alibis and lies. It was most difficult to ferret out the facts."

Sogolov tried to cut the report short. "What did you find out from him, Comrade General?"

"After the most intense interrogation, in which our wills and personalities were pitted against each other, I finally broke him down into a weeping man, fearful of the great people's justice that was about to descend on him."

Kuznetz repeated Sogolov's question. "What did you find out from him, Comrade General?"

"I found out," Hong said snuffing his cigarette out in the ashtray on the desk, "that General Truong Van defected."

Now Kuznetz and Sogolov felt they were getting somewhere. "Then he has gone to the other side?"

"He has," Hong said lighting another cigarette.

"How did this come about?" Kuznetz asked. "And why?"

"There was a plot among several senior officers," Hong said. "Personal profit more than politics made them betray their country. The one exception was Truong Van."

"How does the prisoner—South Vietnamese Colonel Phuong—fit into all this?" Sogolov asked.

"That will be revealed to you presently," Hong said.

"You've performed a valuable service to world socialism," Kuznetz said.

"Thank you, Comrades," Hong replied.

"We would like very much to interview the officers who worked with Truong, if you don't mind," Kuznetz said.

"Impossible."

"Impossible? Why?" Kuznetz asked.

"I had them executed," Hong said.

The expressions on the two Russians' faces was blank, but both were thinking of how Hong himself had covered his own ass in the affair.

"That is unfortunate," Kuznetz said in a strained voice.

"Not to worry, Comrades," Hong assured them. "I saved one for you. The most senior ranking officer involved. Would you care to see him?"

"Please!"

Hong stood up and invited them to follow him.

They left the office and went back down the stairs. The officer who had acted as escort was waiting for them. He saluted, then led the three senior men across the courtyard toward a cell. The firing squad, still waiting to perform their duty, was called to attention. They presented arms.

"Good evening, Comrade Soldiers!" Kuznetz called out in Vietnamese.

Sogolov had to use his native tongue. *Dobri viechier, tovarisch soldat.*"

The squad returned to the position of order arms then were put at ease by their sergeant. Well-dressed in pressed uniforms and shiny boots, they were obviously sharpened up for the Russians' benefit.

The young officer stopped at a cell. After pulling

a large key from his tunic, he opened the door and stepped aside.

"Follow me, please," Hong said.

They went inside a rather pleasant barred room. Although bare, it was clean and well-ventilated. A wooden bunk with a thin mattress and blanket were on one side. A prisoner wearing a striped uniform sat on it. He was hunched over with his head hanging down.

"*Chao ong*," Hong said. "How are you, Doc Nguyek?"

"*Toi manh*," the man answered in a hushed voice.

"Speak Russian out of courtesy for your visitors," Hong instructed him.

"*Da*," Duc answered. "*Kak dela, tavarisch?*"

Hong was angry. "Do not call them comrades, you traitor!"

"I am sorry."

"They wish to hear about Truong Van," Hong said. "I warn you to be candid, Duc."

"*Da*." The prisoner sat up straighter. "Truong Van was a traitor to the People's Socialist Republic of Vietnam. He became a turncoat more than five years ago. He finally reached a decision to do all he could to harm the state. His criminal intent was of such a magnitude that he enlisted others to help him carry out his various plots."

Hong, lighting a cigarette, leaned up against the wall. "Continue, Duc Nguyek. Do not spare us any of the sordid details of this betrayal of the people."

"As you wish," Duc said. "Truong first came into contact with agents from the south when a patriotic

151

intelligence agent compromised a network of spies. Truong had the brave soldier for socialism executed."

Hong looked at the Russians. "That is not the worst!"

Duc took a deep breath. "Then he had the man's family murdered. Even the baby."

"A depraved criminal!" Hong exclaimed.

"Truong befriended the enemy agents and aided them in setting up a spy ring," Duc went on. "He recruited me and I helped to give them many state secrets that were transmitted to the south. They proved harmful to our brave soldiers and their comrades in the Viet Cong during their struggles against the imperialist gangsters."

Hong playfully kicked the man's leg. "Tell the Russian comrades what made Truong defect."

Duc reached down and rubbed his shin, but spoke on. "Truong Van heard that the brave General Hong—"

"That's me!" Hong interrupted.

"—was closing in on him and his criminal activities," Duc said. "We all knew we were lost then. But Truong Van said he could get us out to safety. Thus he made arrangements with a South Vietnamese prisoner to have a friendly reception arranged for him when he defected. He said we could come later. But the brave General Hong was too quick."

Hong dropped his cigarette to the cell floor. He pulled another from the pack and lit it. "You see? I had been working on this case long before you called me in, Comrades. I am a good communist. The KGB should realize that."

152

"We do," Kuznetz said. He didn't believe a word that Duc had spoken. Now he pulled his own rank. "I will question the prisoner, Comrade General Hong."

"Of course," Hong said politely. "That is why I have brought you here."

"I will question him without your presence," Kuznetz added.

"I am happy to oblige you," Hong said with his wide smile. "Please excuse me, Comrades. I will be outside if you need me."

"Thank you," Kuznetz said. He waited until the general withdrew. Then he gestured to Sogolov. "Get to work."

Sogolov walked over and sat down beside the prisoner. "Cigarette?"

Duc silently took one and allowed it to be lit.

The Russian studied the man's face in the match light. He saw a passive, resigned man with all spirit and initiative taken out of him. "Good cigarette, eh?" Sogolov asked. Then he lowered his voice. "It's American—Lucky Strike."

Duc maintained his muteness.

"The comrade general said you were a high-ranking officer," Sogolov said. "What rank did you hold?"

"I was a colonel, Com—, sir."

"It is all right to call me comrade," Sogolov assured him. "My name is Sogolov. Call me Comrade Sogolov if you wish."

Once more Duc sank back into silence.

"I must tell you, Comrade Duc, that I do not believe you are guilty of all those things you said," Sogolov whispered.

Duc said nothing.

"We think that Hong is a hot bag of wind," Sogolov continued. "Why don't you tell us what really happened with the Comrade General Truong Van, eh?"

"Truong Van was a traitor and a spy who dealt with enemies of the people's state," Duc intoned.

"Why are you saying that?"

"I speak the truth," Duc said.

"Who were the enemy agents he and you were supposed to have dealt with?" Sogolov asked.

"I do not know their names," Duc said. "They used codes to identify themselves."

"What codes?"

"I don't remember."

"How would you forget that?" Sogolov demanded to know.

Duc shrugged.

"Where did you have meetings with spies?"

"I am a traitor to the People's Socialist Republic of Vietnam," Duc said.

"Did these agents operate in Hanoi?"

"I passed classified information to the enemies of the People's Socialist Republic of Vietnam," Duc recited.

"How did Truong Van recruit you?"

"I don't remember."

"When did he recruit you?" Sogolov persisted.

"I don't remember."

"What method did Truong Van use to get out of

154

North Vietnam?"

"I am a traitor to the People's Socialist Republic of Vietnam," Duc said again.

Sogolov smiled without humor. He got off the bunk and walked over to Kuznetz. "They've got this noodle-slooping, rice-eating little slant-eyed son of a bitch right where they want him, don't they?"

"It's obvious it's a lost cause," Kuznetz admitted. "We'll get nowhere."

"It would seem it is now time to practice diplomacy, Comrade General," Sogolov said.

"I hate this part of my job," Kuznetz said. He sighed. "Well, let's get it over with."

The two Russians stepped outside the cell where General Hong Kim and the other North Vietnamese officer waited. Kuznetz offered his hand. "Congratulations, Comrade General! You have scored a great victory here in capturing this criminal."

"Thank you!" Hong said beaming. "I trust that your official report will reflect that."

"Of course," Kuznetz assured him.

"Do you wish to question the prisoner any further?" Hong asked.

"No, thank you," Kuznetz said. "We are satisfied."

"Excellent!" Hong motioned to the NVA officer. "He is yours now."

"Yes, Comrade General!"

The officer went inside the cell and emerged, leading Duc by the arm. The prisoner allowed himself to be taken across the courtyard to the opposite wall. He turned and faced outward.

The firing squad was brought to attention by their sergeant. They marched over into position in front of Duc. After being properly aligned, the officer barked the necessary orders.

Seven AK47's belched flames and 7.62 millimeter slugs. Duc's body was jerked violently and thrown against the wall before he collapsed to the courtyard floor.

Hong looked at the Russians. "The people's justice is done."

Kuznetz and Sogolov went back through the heavy door and got into their car. The driver started the engine and began the drive back to the Soviet embassy.

They rode in silence for several moments. Kuznetz finally spoke the obvious. "That bastard Hong coughed up a scapegoat for us."

"Of course," Sogolov said. "He'd been physically tortured and drugged to the point he barely knew up from down. And I imagine his family had been threatened too."

"I suppose, in a strange way, he died satisfied," Kuznetz said. "At least he knew his family would be safe after he made whatever deal was necessary with Hong."

"Now we can't get the truth," Sogolov complained. "To call Hong a liar and a blackmailer would be—" He stopped speaking.

"I know what you are thinking," Kuznetz said sympathetically. "To deny Hong's system of justice would be to deny our own political and social philosophies. He worked within our framework and our

156

methods."

"It is an unfortunate result of communism," Sogolov said.

"Ah, yes," Kuznetz added. "But not all that unusual. Really." He laughed aloud. "After all, dear Comrade Colonel Sogolov, the report on Hong will also clear us of any suspicion too."

"I was thinking of that," Sogolov said with a smile.

Chapter 16

The Black Eagles had penetrated ten kilometers into the wild southern forest area of China on the shores of the Gulf of Tonkin.

When they finally reached a place that seemed adequately isolated, Lieutenant Colonel Falconi ordered a halt in their journey.

One by one, the men joined up with him. "Take a load off your feet, guys," Falconi said. "Settle down and relax a bit. We're going to have a heart-to-heart talk among ourselves."

"Uh oh!" Archie Dobbs said. "It looks like we're in deep shit."

"Yeah," Calvin Culpepper said grinning. "When the old man gets serious, the situation is all fucked up."

Falconi kiddingly nudged Calvin with his boot. "Hey, I really appreciate all the confidence."

"Glad to add to morale, sir," Calvin said.

Falconi looked at the men who had gathered around him. They had formed themselves into a loose semi-circle. Some sat up while others lounged back on their elbows. Paulo Garcia and General Truong Van both leaned up against the same tree off to one side. Lieutenant Ray Swift Elk and Sergeant Major Top Gordon stood behind the group.

"Now you may wonder why I brought you all the way to China for this meeting," Falconi began.

The guys all laughed.

"I'm glad you're in a good mood," the lieutenant colonel said. "Because you're going to need all the humor you can muster up in the next few days."

"Whew!" Blue said. "Maybe I ain't so dawg-fired happy after all!"

"I know," Falconi continued, "that we are in China." He pulled his map from the side pocket of his tiger camouflaged fatigues. "But, unfortunately, that's all I know about our location. This country is not on these beautifully prepared topographical charts that Fagin had issued to us."

General Truong Van carefully observed the Black Eagles as their commander spoke to them. He studied their faces, body movements, and the tone of their voices. They seemed remarkably calm about the dangerous situation they were in. The NVA officer could not decide if they were incredibly brave, very confident, or amazingly suicidal.

"Our main task—hell, the *only* task—is to exfiltrate out of China as quickly as possible," Falconi said. "Without a proper OPLAN or maps, it is going to be what the learned masters of military science would term an 'operation of opportunity'."

"I know another name for it, sir," Archie said. "In the Air Force they call it flying by the seat of your pants."

"Well said, Archie," Falconi agreed. "Because that is exactly what we're going to do. The bottom line is that we are in an enemy country. There are no friendly lines nearby. We have no safehouses to hide in. And nobody knows we're here that could help us."

159

Paulo, the commo expert, added, "We couldn't talk to 'em at this distance anyway, sir."

"Add the fact that we don't even know what lies over the next hill, and it's almost the blind leading the blind," Falconi went on. "We've got to work big on reconnaissance. Without it, we're just stumbling around in the dark. We've got to poke ahead, peek around, check things out, then make our moves. And I mean that applies to every goddamned single meter we've got to travel. Each valley, stretch of woods, and other terrain features could be concealing something dangerous to us. Even a single paddy-wading peasant could work to compromise us."

Sergeant Major Top Gordon entered the conversation. "That brings up noise discipline. We're all damned good at sneaking-and-peeking. We're ace high on camouflage, but I got to tell you guys something. Our noise discipline sucks. Let's work extra hard on keeping quiet. Tape down anything on you that rattles, and keep talking down to a minimum while we're on the move."

"Good point, Sergeant Major," Falconi said.

Gunnar Olson scratched his blond head. "What about killing unfriendly folks we run across, sir?"

"Hopefully, we won't bump into anybody," Falconi answered. "And vice-versa. But if we do spot anybody, we'll avoid them like the plague."

"What about pussy, sir?" Archie asked with a leer. "Maybe if I used my masculine charms to seduce some Chinese broad—"

"Forget it, Archie," Malpractice McCorckel said. "You couldn't make it with any of the broads

160

around here with a duffel bag full of yuan."

"Oh, yeah?" Archie countered. "I'll bet I could with a duffel bag full of egg-foo-yung."

"Archie," Malpractice said. "I ain't got any medicine for the Chinese version of the clap."

"Then it's settled," Falconi said with a wink. "No lovemaking, guys. Sorry." He pointed to Archie. "So you forget the women and concentrate on scouting. We'll be depending on you, Archie."

"Right on, sir."

Falconi raised his gaze to the others. "But Archie can't do it all. He'll be exhausted if he has to man the point all hours of the day. So we're going to break down into two-man point teams. One guy will do the compass and route-following work while the other provides security for him."

Ray Swift Elk raised his hand. "Any particular direction we're going to travel, sir?"

"Even without a map I know the direction to the ocean is south. So that's our azimuth guys—one-eight-zero."

"I reckon you're right, sir," Top said. "Over water seems the best escape route."

"If we find a fishing village, we should be able to steal a boat," Falconi said. "With luck it'll a powered one with a motor of sorts."

Blue grinned. "Don't worry about nothin' sir. I'm a sailor and proud of it. If it's got oars, sails, or an engine, I'll get her out to sea and navigate us back home."

"Hey," Paulo Garcia interjected. "How the hell do you think I used to go tuna fishing out of San Diego? By Amtrack? I can sail too."

161

"Then we're in great shape," Falconi said. "And that's the plan. Head south and find the ocean. Then find a village and a boat. After that we'll let Captain Blue Richards and his first mate Paulo cruise us back to our side of this war." He pointed to Gunnar and Malpractice. "You two guys are the first point-team."

"Hey!" Top snapped. "What're you waiting for? Let's move the hell outta here!"

Colonel Huong and Lieutenant Anh ate slowly, savoring the rice and fresh fish. The meal would have been perfect if a few vegetables had been available, but life aboard the patrol boat was as austere as in the field. If it hadn't been for a lucky catch by one of the sailors fishing while off watch, the menu would have consisted only of boiled rice and weak tea.

The cabin door opened and the captain entered the small cabin. "We have made contact with a Chinese torpedo boat, Comrades."

Huong stopped eating. "What is our position in relation to the coast of China?"

"We are fifty kilometers away," the captain assured him. "This vessel is well within international waters."

"Let us hope our Chinese comrades mean no mischief," Huong said. Like all NVA intelligence officers, he was well aware of the strained relations between his own country and Red China.

"The Chinese captain is making no overt hostile moves," the patrol boat skipper said. "He has re-

162

quested that we meet with him."

"Does that mean he wishes to come aboard?" Anh asked.

"Yes, Comrade."

"Can we avoid that?" Huong wanted to know.

"Alas, no," the captain said. "It would be considered an insult and would make him suspicious. His reaction would be a violent one."

Huong smiled. "Then let us welcome the comrade."

The three officers stepped out of the cabin and onto the cockpit deck. Anh, as an act of military courtesy, allowed the two senior officers to precede him up the ladder leading to the flying bridge. A sailor stood at the railing, peering intently through a powerful set of binoculars toward the horizon.

"Have you sighted the Chinese vessel yet, Comrade sailor?" the skipper asked.

"*Kong co*, Comrade Captain," the sailor said making a negative reply.

The officer-of-the deck stepped forward. "Our radio room has reported intermittent contact with the Chinese torpedo boat, Comrade Captain," he reported. "Their transmissions are powerful. All indications are that they are continuing on an interception course with us."

Colonel Huong spat over the side in disgust. "The Chinese squabble with the Soviet comrades on their borders, yet the Russians give them more support in communications and other technical equipment than they give us."

"We all agree with you, Comrade Colonel," Anh said. "That is the main reason we are participating

163

in this particular operation."

"Indeed!" the boat captain agreed.

"Unidentified vessel off the starboard bow," the sailor with the binoculars sang out. "Approaching steadily."

"Can you make out its colors?" the captain asked.

"Only a red flag on the stern," the sailor said. He continued his vigilance uninterrupted for another ten minutes. "A Chinese vessel, Comrade Captain. Motor torpedo boat."

The next half hour dragged slowly by as the small ship eased along on its course. Finally, when the red flag with the large gold star and four smaller ones was visible with the naked eye, the North Vietnamese skipper ordered his own vessel to stop the engine. The Chinese made a shallow turn, then lined up and came straight ahead. When they were gunwale-to-gunwale, their crewmen tossed lines aboard the North Vietnamese boat.

The Chinese captain, smiling broadly, waved from his own flying bridge. "*Tso-shan*, Comrades," he called out. "May I have permission to come aboard?"

"Of course, Comrade," the North Vietnamese said with feigned politeness. He did not fail to notice the Chinese sailors manning the heavy machine guns on both bow and stern. A quick order from their skipper would cause heavy slugs to rake the North Vietnamese boat without mercy.

The Chinese leaped aboard. He turned and saluted the flag on the stern. He next turned and rendered a salute to the captain. "How kind of you to invite me!"

"Please, let us go below to the cabin for refreshments," the North Vietnamese captain invited. "I am Lien."

"And I am Mung," the Chinese said.

Both Colonel Huong and Lieutenant Anh then introduced themselves and exchanged salutes.

"This way, please," Lien said leading the officers down the ladder to the cockpit. A sailor there opened the cabin door and they all went inside.

Lien went to a small cabinet on the port side. He opened it and produced some glasses and a bottle. "Polish vodka," he announced.

He poured glasses for everyone present. When he'd finished, he raised his own. "To world socialism!"

The others dutifully responded to the toast.

The glasses were refilled.

"To the struggle against imperialism," Mung said.

Again the officers drank.

Next Lien toasted Red China. Then Mung toasted North Vietnam. When the glasses were again filled, Lien indicated there might be more alcoholic salutes by placing the vodka within easy reach.

Mung took a small sip of his. "The weather for the previous two weeks has been a sailor's delight."

"Most assuredly," Lien said.

Mung looked at Huong and Anh. His smile widened. "I am curious as to why army officers are on the high seas."

"We have been attached to the people's navy as

165

observers," Huong said. He quickly added. "It is hoped our military knowledge will expand through exposure with the war being carried on at sea."

"Yes," Anh said. "Our country is actually *fighting* the Yankee imperialists." The sarcasm seemed to drip from his cold voice.

Mung still grinned. "And well appreciated by all the other socialist countries, Comrade. You may recall that we did so in Korea a few years ago." He treated himself to another drink. "Actually you are three boats, are you not?"

"A small squadron actually," Lien said. "I am honored to have been appointed commander."

"A well deserved honor I am sure," Mung remarked. "Are you on any specific mission?"

"Patrol duties only," Lien assured him.

"Aren't you even assigned a zone? Or perhaps courses to follow, such as a triangle?" Mung asked.

"Where we go is my prerogative, Comrade," Lien said.

"Your superiors display great faith in your command ability," Mung said. "How very flattering to you."

"I am a North Vietnamese naval officer," Lien said.

"You are most worthy allies," Mung said. He finished his drink and set the glass down.

Lien immediately filled it. "A sincere host is disturbed by the sight of empty cups and bowls."

"That is a Chinese proverb," Mung said.

"You Chinese are a perceptive and descriptive people," Lien said.

"Thank you." Mung pointed out a porthole. "I

also noticed a helicopter landing pad on one of your boats." He laughed. "And there was a helicopter on it."

"I certainly hope so," Lien said. "My superiors' trust in my devotion to duty would be sorely tried if I should lose it."

Mung laughed at the joke. "I am sure." His face grew serious. "But why do you carry this aerial support with you?"

"The American Navy has a heavy presence in the Gulf of Tonkin," Colonel Huong said. "The helicopter may come in handy if we confront the imperialist gangsters."

"Yes," Mung agreed. "An Mi-24 gunship is a formidable addition to one's squadron." He set the glass down again, this time signaling a refusal for a refill. "I must return to my own vessel, Comrades. Like you, I also have my duties and obligations."

A reverse procedure brought the officers back up on the flying bridge. After another exchange of salutes and handshakes, Captain Mung leaped back to the sidedeck. When he climbed back onto the flying bridge, the North Vietnamese sailors cast off the lines they had received. With another wave, the Chinese pulled away, turning north toward their own coast.

Captain Mung looked back over the stern at the North Vietnamese boat. His executive officer also glared at the vessel. "What are they doing in these waters, Comrade Captain?"

"I do not know," Mung said. "But I am sure it is for some devious reason. They are up to no good."

167

"What will do we do?" the exec asked.

"We will hang back and shadow those devious devils."

Gunnar Olson crept forward through the forest. He noticed the change in the types of vegetation in that terrain. The brush and trees were more like a regular woods back in his home state of Minnesota rather than the dense jungle of Vietnam. He stopped long enough to consult his compass to make sure he was staying on the southeast course that Lieutenant Colonel Falconi had decreed.

Malpractice McCorckel, carrying Archie Dobbs' Prick-Six radio, followed closely behind Gunnar, but he wasn't interested in the azimuth they followed. His job was to provide security for the Norwegian-American, so Gunnar could concentrate on going the correct route. Malpractice kept his eyes moving and his ears tuned for any sounds that suggested even the slightest hint of danger.

"Hold it, Gunnar!" he suddenly whispered.

Gunnar immediately stopped and squatted down.

Malpractice listened for several more minutes. Then he spoke into the radio. "Falcon, this is Point. Over."

Falconi's voice responded to the call.

"We've got a disturbance off to the northeast," Malpractice reported. "I think it's worth taking a look. Over."

"Roger," Falconi agreed. "I'll send Blue up. Out."

Three minutes later, Blue Richards came forward

168

and joined the other two Black Eagles on the point. "What's got y'all so jumpy?"

"Just listen," Malpractice said.

The three listened intently for several minutes. Blue pulled some chewing tobacco out of his jacket pocket. "I don't hear nothin'," he said taking a chaw.

"It don't go on all the time," Gunnar said. "It just comes and goes. You got to take some time. I didn't hear it at first either."

"Okay, boys," Blue said. "Let's give these ears of our'n a real workout."

It was ten full minutes before a distant, low-toned swish was heard. Now Blue was interested. "I think all these trees are distorting the noise. We need to move closer."

"Let's go," Gunnar said.

"Sure 'nuff," Blue said. "Let's go!"

The three spread out a bit, holding their weapons at the ready as they moved through the trees. Malpractice ordered a halt a couple of times. On those occurrences, one of them would move forward to check out the area ahead. Then he would return and signal the others to resume the search.

Suddenly the noise sounded again. This time it was definitely louder and closer. Blue frowned in puzzlement. "I'll tell ya, I cain't figger that one out. What about you two fellers?"

"It's something swooshing," Gunnar said. He shrugged. "I guess that ain't much help, is it?"

"Try to think of things that 'swoosh'," Malpractice suggested.

They pondered the problem for several moments.

169

Blue motioned them to follow him. "Piss on it! Let's go eyeball whatever it is."

Once again they moved northward. The woods seemed to thin a bit. This caused them a small amount of alarm as the cover lessened, but the next time they heard the noise it was plainer. Louder and deeper than before, it seemed to rise up, peak, then quickly fade away. Then it did it again—three times in succession.

"We all know what that is," Blue said. "C'mon!"

They only had to go another thirty meters before they found the road. Well-graded and heavily traveled, it cut through the woods as straight as an arrow.

"Whoever put that in, knew exactly where he wanted it go," Malpractice said.

The noise sounded in the distance. The Black Eagles dropped down and waited. Within a few minutes, two heavy trucks of the Chinese army sped past. Malpractice got on his radio and reported what they'd found. Falconi's reply was terse and direct:

"Point, avoid that place at all costs. Turn onto a direct southerly route. Let me know when we can get on the move again. Send Blue back to the main body. Out."

They retraced their steps until Gunnar and Malpractice were once more in position to act as point for the small column. Blue hurried back to report to Lieutenant Colonel Falconi.

Gunnar checked his compass, then stepped out due south. He moved slowly in the correct direction, making continuous compass checks to make sure he didn't veer off from the correct azimuth. But fifteen minutes later he stopped and beckoned to Malpractice to join him.

"What's up?" Malpractice whispered.

"Look!" Gunnar pointed at a spot ten meters in front of him.

"God!" Malpractice exclaimed. He moved forward and squatted down to study the ground. He was on top of a well-worn trail, with hundreds of footprints going in both directions. He wasted no time in getting back on the radio. "Falcon, this is Point. Come up here quick. Out."

This time it was Falconi and Archie who showed up to see what was going on. When they saw the trail, they grimaced. Archie rubbed his hand across his dirty face. "That place has got more traffic than downtown Boston during the rush hour."

"This is some real bad shit," Falconi admitted. "Gunnar, Malpractice, wait here. Archie and I are going to move around here a bit and see what the hell the score is."

The pair went south down the trail. They stayed off the soft dirt to avoid having their own footprints appear so obviously with the smaller, different Chinese variety.

"Have you noticed any tracks off in the woods?" Falconi asked.

"No, sir," Archie answered. "The people that move along here don't want to get snagged in bushes."

"You know what that means," Falconi said. "They're not concerned about security and cover.

171

That could be a plus for us."

"It sure could," Archie said. "If those—"

The sound of voices abruptly broke over the scene. The two Black Eagles made silent dives into the bushes. They waited tensely for several minutes. Then a Red Chinese Army patrol sauntered by. The men talked loudly, carrying their weapons in a careless manner.

After they went past, Falconi and Archie chanced a further investigation down the track. They found three sites of former bivouacs before they finally stopped.

Falconi sighed. "This situation is worse than I thought."

"I think I would term what we've got here as 'wall-to-wall Chinese troops'," Archie said.

Chapter 17

Fagin laid down the microphone and took off the earphones. "I give up," he said in a strained, hoarse voice.

The submarine radio operator was sympathetic. "Too bad they don't have a CW radio, Mister Fagin. We could set up an automated transmission that would keep going until they answered."

Fagin shook his head. "I don't think it would do any good. If they're not responding to voice, they wouldn't be able to come back to us under any circumstances." He cleared his throat. "Damn! My vocal cords are worn out."

"I'm not surprised," the radio man said. "You've been talking into that mike for twelve straight hours. I'll take over for awhile, if you'd like."

"I appreciate that," Fagin said. "But it's useless." He stood up and stepped out into the passageway. "You've been a great help."

"I was happy to lend a hand, Mister Fagin," the submariner said. "If you decide to try again, just let me know."

"Right," Fagin said. He made his way through the submarine to the control room. "Is the skipper around?"

The exec looked up from where he was peering over the radarman's shoulder. "He's off watch, Mister Fagin. You'll find him in his cabin. Any luck?"

"Not a bit," Fagin said. He stepped through the hatch and walked a few paces down to the captain's quarters. He leaned inside. "Howdy, Mac."

"Hello, Chuck," Commander Lucas MacIntyre said. He looked at the CIA man's face. "You don't bring any good news, do you?"

"I'm afraid not," Chuck said.

MacIntyre gestured to his bunk. "Sit down. It appears it is decision-reaching time, huh?"

"I'd say so," Fagin said accepting the invitation.

"Okay," MacIntyre said turning his full attention to his old friend. "The situation has boiled down to this: Lieutenant Colonel Robert Falconi led his Black Eagle Detachment into the North Vietnamese territory to link up and exfiltrate a high-ranking NVA general who wanted to defect."

"Right," Fagin said. "The operation was well-planned and checked out through a South Vietnamese colonel who had recently escaped from imprisonment up there through the efforts of the general you mentioned."

"But that colonel killed himself, right?" MacIntyre asked.

"Yeah. Which made me very very nervous about this whole thing."

"At any rate, Falconi and his guys went ashore," MacIntyre said. "We assume he got the

174

general from the code he broadcast to me prior to executing the exfiltration. Then he made his move to come out to this boat for the trip home."

"Yeah," Fagin said. "Except the operation then went completely to hell when a couple of North Vietnamese patrol boats appeared in the area."

"And since then we've made an exhaustive effort on the radio to contact Falconi," MacIntyre said. "To no avail."

Fagin sighed. "So let's wrap it up, Mac. I'll write my report. The Black Eagles are cooked geese—gone goslings—they've had it."

"Do you want to turn about and head back for South Vietnam?" MacIntyre asked.

"Let's do it," Fagin said getting up. "I'll start my report."

Captain Mung, skipper of the Red Chinese Navy's motor torpedo boat number 14, peered through his large binoculars. His steady gaze swept the horizon. Mung turned to the watch officer at his side on the flying bridge. "Have there been sightings of any kind?"

"No, Comrade *Sheung-Kaau*," the officer, a lieutenant named Chiang replied. "The sea has remained empty."

Mung took another look. "Those Vietnamese are up to something. There is no doubt about that. I have sent a message back to port headquarters to report their activities."

"It is too bad we have nothing to add," the other officer said.

175

"Yes," Chiang said. He put his binoculars on the control console. "But three armed boats and a helicopter gunship are doing more than routine patrolling."

"I do not trust those southern bastards," Chiang said in a blunt fashion.

"I agree," Mung said. "There have been border clashes before, but lately the situation has been escalating to alarming proportions."

"Perhaps the North Vietnamese think their war with the Americans has made them invincible," the other Chinese officer said.

"They are getting big heads all right," Mung agreed. "They don't seem to realize that the American soldiers and Marines are being forced to fight with one hand tied behind their backs. If the United States government unleashed their full power, the Yankees would roll out of Vietnam and come clear up to Peking."

Chiang laughed. "If the North Vietnamese want to fight us, they'll find us much less inclined to hamstring our army and navy."

"We would crush the little weasels," Mung added. "Our two cultures have hundreds of years of fighting each other. The only reason we never conquered them was because the great Chinese people were never united as one great nation before."

The boat's radio operator scampered up the ladder to the flying bridge. "Comrade *Sheung-Kaau!*"

The captain, very interested in what the communications specialist would have to report, turned and gave him his full attention. "Yes, Comrade?"

"I have been making a security sweep of all frequencies, Comrade Captain," the radioman said. "All have been normal transmissions except for one. It is a continual broadcast of beeps."

Chiang glanced at the captain. "I would not be surprised if the strange sounds had something to do with those North Vietnamese boats."

"I agree. I will go below to listen," Mung said. He nodded to Chiang. "Take over the bridge, Lieutenant."

"Yes, Comrade *Sheung-Kaau*."

The captain hurried down the ladder with the radio operator on his heels. When they reached the commo room, they went inside. The seaman switched on the speaker. The sounds were a high-pitched BEEP-BEEP, BEEP, BEEP-BEEP.

Mung listened to the transmissions. "They follow a pattern, do they not?"

"Yes, Comrade Captain," the radioman said. "They have not varied in all the time I have monitored them."

"What do you think they are?" Mung asked.

The sailor shrugged. "I do not recognize any meaning in them, Comrade *Sheung-Kaau*. They are not Morse code so convey no message to me."

"Of course." Mung realized the man's training was severely limited. All the people's navy required was that he be able to send and receive transmissions of the simplest nature. The Red Chinese government did not relish the idea of having numerous communications experts with the

177

potential of creating dangerous mischief.

The transmissions continued uninterrupted. BEEP-BEEP, BEEP, BEEP-BEEP.

"Do they never cease?" Mung asked.

"They have gone on steadily, Comrade Captain," the radio operator said. "The person broadcasting must have a tireless finger on the key."

"You have never heard these signals before? Not even during your training?" Mung inquired.

The sailor shook his head. "No, Comrade *Sheung-Kaau*."

Mung was thoughtful for several moments. "Go to the flying bridge and have Lieutenant Chiang report here to me. He is a graduate of the Maritime Academy and he has recently returned for further courses. Perhaps he can enlighten me."

"Yes, Comrade Captain."

It took the eager junior lieutenant no more than five minutes to have himself properly relieved by a chief petty officer. As soon as that was accomplished, he rushed to the radio room and made his appearance. "I am reporting as ordered, Comrade Captain."

Mung nudged the radio operator. "Turn on the speaker."

Chiang stood listening for several moments. His face remained impassive as if there was nothing unusual about the affair. He was puzzled. "What is it you wish of me, Comrade Captain?"

"Can you identify that type of broadcast?" Mung asked.

"Yes, of course, Comrade *Sheung-Kaau*. They are radio direction transmissions." He peered in-

178

tently at the equipment. "They are evidently coming from the north. From our own mainland."

Mung, an unsophisticated officer who had earned his rank in earlier, simpler days, shook his head. "I still do not fully comprehend this."

"The transmissions are an aid to show where they are coming from," Chiang explained. "For example, in navigation, if two stations are broadcasting such signals, the receiver could pinpoint his exact location by drawing lines on a map following the azimuth he finds the signals the strongest. Where those lines cross is where he is positioned."

"Then this is a navigational aid?" Mung asked.

The sailor volunteered his own opinion. "I think not, Comrade Captain. There is only one set of signals."

"That is true," Chiang said. "It would not be possible to use that for locating oneself."

"Then what use would they be?" Mung asked getting impatient.

"If one wished to know the location of the broadcaster, all he has to do is find the direction of the strongest signal and go on that course," Chiang said. "For example if a downed pilot had such a device, his rescuers could go straight to him in a minimum amount of time." Suddenly the lieutenant's eyes opened wide as another thought entered his mind. "Or if an enemy agent wished to meet with someone, he could let them home in on him by following the transmissions."

Mung was delighted. "Now we know why those Vietnamese weasels are skulking about here. We

179

will follow them *and* the signals. Come, Comrade Lieutenant Chiang, you and I will be spending more hours on the bridge before this affair is over." He looked at the radio operator. "Send a message to our base. Inform them of the situation and request additional boats to assist us."

"Yes, Comrade *Sheung-Kaau!*"

Colonel Huong wished he hadn't eaten so much as he sat in the bow of the small launch. It bounced and rolled with each wave as it was driven across the space between the command patrol boat and the vessel with the helicopter pad. The colonel glanced over at Lieutenant Anh, envying the young officer for his strong stomach.

"Coi churng!" Anh cried. "There is the helicopter now!"

Huong looked toward the northern horizon and could see the black image of the approaching aircraft. He gestured to the sailor controlling the launch's rudder and throttle. "Cannot this small vessel go faster?"

"Toi tec," the sailor responded apologetically. "I have the speed turned to maximum now, Comrade Colonel."

Huong endured more of the bouncing until they finally came alongside the boat with the helicopter landing pad. By the time he and Anh scrambled aboard, the chopper was coming in for a landing. The aircraft's crew barely waited for the rotors to stop turning before they rushed forward to secure the helicopter to the pad. Unlike dry land operations, there was always the danger that a sudden swell could cause the mother boat to list enough to send the valuable machine skidding off into the ocean.

The pilot stepped out of the aircraft and came forward to report to the two army officers. "There is much activity to the north, Comrades," he said.

"What have you seen?" Huong asked.

"Several Chinese torpedo motor boats are approaching this area," the pilot said.

"I knew that son of a Peking whore was suspicious!" Huong declared referring to the Chinese captain. He started to volunteer to go for a personal viewing of the situation, but decided his stomach was not up for it. "Comrade Lieutenant Anh!"

"Yes, Comrade Colonel?"

"I want you to go with the comrade pilot for a reconnaissance of the situation," Huong said. "Count the number of Chinese vessels and watch them for awhile. See if you can figure out their intentions."

"Yes, Comrade Colonel."

The pilot motioned to his crew. "Refill the fuel tank. I am going out again."

Within a quarter of an hour, the Soviet Mi-24 Hind-D helicopter's rotors bit the air and lifted the craft up. A push by the pilot on the cyclic stick and the chopper swept northward over the Gulf of Tonkin.

Lieutenant Anh sat in the gunner's cockpit in front of the pilot. They could easily speak through the intercom as the pilot went for more altitude.

After reached eight thousand feet, he went into a forward movement heading toward the position he last saw the Chinese boats.

Anh tried to use his binoculars, but the shaking of the Mi-24 made their use difficult. He relied on his unassisted eyesight as they flew on through the brilliant afternoon sky. Finally, after fifteen minutes, the pilot spoke over the intercom:

"Comrade Lieutenant! There on the horizon at one o'clock."

Anh, unused to being in the air, had a bad time in locating anything to see. But finally he could make out the specks. As the chopper drew closer, the objects gradually formed shape until they were obviously boats.

"How close do you want to go, Comrade Lieutenant?" the pilot asked.

"Just a bit closer," Anh answered. "Then I wish to observe them."

The Chinese boats moved steadily through the water, leaving slight white wakes at their stern. Even Anh could tell they were not at full speed, though the courses they followed were straight and seemed purposeful.

A few more minutes passed, then the Chinese closed together more. After a bit more maneuvering they were very close, appearing to be within hailing distance of each other.

"Comrade Lieutenat," the pilot said. "There is another boat off on the horizon."

"Does it appear to be alone? Anh asked unable to find it in what seemed an endless sea.

"It *is* alone," the pilot said. "Can you not see

the vessel, Comrade Lieutenant?"

"Of course I can see the accursed Chinese boat," Anh lied in anger. "Let us go take a close look at it."

"How close, Comrade Lieutenant?"

"I want to see the sailors' faces," Anh said sarcastically.

"With pleasure, Comrade Lieutenant!" He used both collective and cyclic to make a quick, stomach-churning—for Anh—descent. Then the pilot went into a power dive. Straightening out just above the water, he pointed the nose down for maximum horizontal speed.

Anh regretted his brash words about looking into the countenances of Chinese seamen, but he said nothing as they streaked toward the boat. When they flashed past, the lieutenant didn't notice the crew as much as he did their anti-aircraft gun mounted on the stern.

The pilot, having a hell of a good time, pulled up in a maneuver that made Anh think he'd left his asshole a thousand feet below. "Another look, Comrade Lieutenant?"

"Not at that boat," Anh said weakly. "Let us take a slow deliberate viewing of the entire scene."

"You are positive you do not wish—"

"I said a *slow, deliberate* look at all the boats!" Anh interrupted in a flash of nervous anger.

The pilot's voice showed his disappointment. "Very well, Comrade Lieutenant."

They spent the next half hour slowly cruising back and forth watching the Chinese go about

183

their business. Finally Anh had seen all he needed and ordered the helicopter to return to the mother boat.

Anh endured some sharp banking and belly-churning maneuvering as the pilot amused himself during the return flight. By the time they settled down on the landing pad, the lieutenant was more than ready to slip out of the gunner's seat and settle down into the cabin with Colonel Huong.

The colonel was anxious to hear what he'd observed. "Quickly, Anh! What are the Chinese up to?"

"Three more boats are converging on the one who visited us," Anh said. "It is obvious they wish to form a squadron and shadow us. Their position is just over the horizon to the north."

"Are you sure it was the same Chinese boat that contacted us?" Huong asked.

"*Co*, Comrade Colonel! I saw the captain's face as we sped overhead," Anh said. "I also noticed their armament which they did not have displayed when they made their call on us."

"What sort of arms?" Huong asked.

"Anti-aircraft machine guns," Anh said. "They are quad-mounted and easily capable of blasting our helicopter out of the sky. They also had their torpedo tubes uncovered."

Huong angrily clenched his fists. "They could blow us out of the water. I fear that any attempt to rescue General Huong Van will result in his death."

"And also the death of the Black Eagles," Anh reminded him. "And even the comrade general

184

was willing to die for that."

Huong calmed down a bit. "Yes. Either we will accomplish the mission by bringing about the destruction of Falconi and his men, or the Chinese will."

Anh shrugged. "Either way Falconi dies. Who cares?"

Fagin sat at the desk in the cubbyhole of a cabin that had been provided for him on the *Perch*. Wadded up pieces of paper that had been angrily thrown to the deck showed the difficulty he was having in writing the report.

This document was addressed in a manner to go through Brigadier General James Taggart to SOG Headquarters. From there a copy was to be passed on to CIA Staff Directory of Southeast Asia. Fagin hated composing those words which detailed his estimate of the destruction of the Black Eagles. He could only suggest they had either been killed or captured wholly or individually in a botched exfiltration operation.

Commander Lucas MacIntyre appeared in the door. "How's it going, Chuck?"

"Shitty, Mac," Fagin answered. He gestured at all the wasted paper. "Maybe it's because I just plain hate to write those goddamned words 'Black Eagle Detachment destroyed'. Hell! I even hate to say 'em."

"I've already turned in my after-action statement," MacIntyre said. "But I'd be glad to help you with yours. I'll even give you an endorsement

185

that pure misadventure fucked up the operation. It was well planned out."

"Ah, hell," Fagin said. "I don't give a damn about getting an ass chewing. It just makes me sick that after all these missions things have finally come to a halt."

"What'll the CIA and SOG do?" MacIntyre asked.

"Form another unit," Fagin said. "But let me tell you something, Mac. I've been in this game for more than twenty-five years, and there never has been and never will be an outfit like Robert Falconi's Black Eagles. They're one in a million."

"That's what I've heard too," MacIntyre said. "I suppose he did everything he could to get his guys out of there."

"Yeah," Fagin agreed. "If there was any trick, scheme, or cockeyed idea that was worth a try, Falconi would go for it. Why short of going to Red China, he would probably have—" Fagin stopped speaking.

"What's the matter?" MacIntyre asked.

"Red China? Do you suppose that magnificent son of a bitch would have turned north instead of south?" Fagin asked. "Would Falconi be wild enough to try to use Red China itself as an exfiltration point?"

MacIntyre flatly answered, "Yes!"

"We didn't check north, did we?" Falconi said leaping up. He grabbed MacIntyre by his shirt front. "Mac, we got to try it. What do you say?"

Commander MacIntyre, grinning, freed himself and went to the intercom on the wall. He turned it to the control room. "Now hear this!" he said loudly. "Now hear this! Prepare to change course. Come about to zero-zero-five."

Chapter 18

Malpractice McCorckel checked his watch. After noting the time he hurried forward. "Gunnar!"

Gunnar Olson stopped and turned around. "Yeah?"

"Our stint on the point is over," Malpractice said. "We've got to wait for Blue and Buffalo Soldier."

"Whew!" Gunnar said. "It's about time. I'm wore out from breaking trail."

"It would have been worse in the jungle," Malpractice pointed out. "And hotter too."

A slight rustling sign behind them caught their attention. Blue Richards and Calvin "Buffalo Soldier" Culpepper came through the brush. Blue showed his lazy grin. "How y'all boys doin'?"

"Okay," Malpractice said. "Glad to see you."

"I'll bet," Calvin said. "Anything special to tell us before we take over?"

"Yeah," Gunnar said. "We keep running into more signs of Chinese troop activity. They're pretty careless in comparison to the NVA down south."

"Well, they ain't engaged in an open war," Blue

said.

"Yeah," Malpractice agreed. He handed the Prick-Six radio over to Calvin. "But that don't mean they won't turn nasty if they spot us. So go slow and easy."

"You betcha," Blue said. "Y'all git on back and take it easy in the column for awhile."

Malpractice and Gunnar, walking slow with fatigue, returned to rejoin the main body of the unit. Blue eyed Calvin carefully. "Want to flip for point?"

"Sure." He pulled out a coin and flipped it into the air. "Call it, Blue."

"Heads," Blue said before it hit the ground.

They bent down and looked at it. Calvin grinned. "I'll take security." He slipped the radio over his shoulder.

"Mmm," Blue said. "How about two outta three?"

"Nope," Calvin said cradling his M16 rifle in his hands. "But don't fret none, my man. I'll keep a sharp eye out."

"Pardon me," Blue said in a surly tone, "while I consult Mister Compass to see which direction south is." Blue checked for the proper azimuth, then stepped off into a slow walk. "Gulf of Tonkin, here we come," he said.

Leading a unit through unknown enemy territory is hard work. Blue and Calvin settled into the task, giving their particular responsibilities hard concentration. An hour slipped by as the two moved slowly in the proper direction. Calvin stayed behind his partner, ready to cover him in the event of encounters with Chinese troops.

Blue suddenly stopped.

"Hey!" Calvin whispered looking around in agitated movements. "What's happening?"

"Looky here." Blue bent down and picked up a document from the ground. "A Chinese magazine."

Calvin looked at it. "Yeah. I wonder what it says?"

Blue flipped through it looking for pictures of women.

"You're looking at it backward, man," Calvin said grinning.

"What the hell are you talkin' about?"

"Them Chinamen read from right to left," Calvin explained. "So they're magazines open from the opposite end of ours."

"So who gives a shit?" Blue remarked still looking for women. "Damn! the onliest broads in here is wearing blue coveralls."

Calvin laughed. "That's prob'ly why some Chinese soldier threw it away."

"Yeah? Well, speakin' o' Chinese soljers, we'd better take a look around here," Blue said.

The two spread out a bit and checked the area. It was Calvin who found what they were looking for. "Hey, Blue," he called out in a stage whisper. "Over here."

Blue came over and noted the spot where several people had been sitting around. The grass was mashed flat and there were cigarette butts thrown around. Calvin found a couple of wet places several paces away. "A couple of 'em took a piss over here," he said.

"I wonder if they went together," Blue said.

"I wonder if they was holding hands," Calvin added with a grin. "Well, there ain't no doubt that these woods is full of 'em huh? We're going through a place where the Chinese are running regular patrols."

"Now don't that make you want to be careful?" Blue said. "C'mon, we got to find the ocean so's we can git a boat and skedaddle outta here."

While Calvin and Blue worked hard at the head of the column, General Truong Van was having a relatively easy time in the middle of it. He checked his radio directional transmitter from time to time, to make sure it was still broadcasting signals. He clicked it off during long periods of inaction, figuring that if it were being monitored, the listeners would have pinpointed his position before the stop in activity.

The NVA general glanced at Paulo who walked beside him. "Has anyone figured out our exact location yet?"

Paulo shook his head. "I'm afraid not, General. Falconi just figures if we keep moving south, we'll eventually run into the Gulf of Tonkin."

Truong nodded. "An amazing man."

"I gotta tell you," Paulo said. "I've never seen an officer like him in the Marine Corps. Our folks are trained mostly to work within the framework of naval support and procedures. Even force recon don't go out for long periods of complete isolation. But guys outta the army's Green Berets are born and bred to fight alone and stay alone."

"And even to die alone," Truong added.

"True, General," Paulo said. "And now I'm one of 'em."

"I would assume that Colonel Falconi does not like a lot of meddling in his operations," Truong said.

"That's right," Paulo said. "Once we was up to our necks in NVA—that's your boys, General—and the brass told Falconi to get his ass outta there. He told 'em to stick it. He don't go into no place just to run."

"He is running now," Truong pointed out.

"Yeah," Paulo said with a grin. "But he's got your ass, ain't he?"

"Yes," Truong said. "He most assuredly does."

"If I was you, General," Paulo said seriously. "I wouldn't forget that."

Truong sank back into his personal thoughts. He had to consider what to do if the Chinese caught the detachment. The first thing, of course, would be to suddenly get Garcia's weapon and turn it on Falconi. The other Black Eagles would shoot him down, but that was actually preferable to falling into Chinese hands.

If Truong's own men— Colonel Huong and Lieutenant Anh—hit the Black Eagles, they will not hold back for his personal safety. They will blast away until not a man of Falconi's is left standing. Even if Truong dies in the crossfire, so

192

be it.

Either way, the NVA general thought, the Black Eagles will be cut off, surrounded, and outnumbered. They won't stand a chance.

Truong's black thoughts occupied his mind, but up ahead Blue Richards' own mental faculties were on full alert. He stopped for a moment, then began descending into a wooden valley, walking slowly. Calvin Culpepper, right on his heels, followed. "Slow down, blue," he urged him. "Remember you got seven guys and an NVA general strung out behind you."

"Yeah," Blue said. "Plus a crotchety army sergeant right on my ass."

"I am here for your comfort and protection," Calvin joked.

"Yeah? Then give me a cold beer," Blue insisted.

They reached the bottom of the shallow valley. Blue, knowing that the group would take more time to get there, followed Calvin's advice and tuned the already slow pace down to a snail's speed. They began the ascent to reach the other side. It took ten minutes. When they reached there they found themselves in a tangle of thick woods.

"I can't see shit," Blue complained.

"We might have to go around," Calvin suggested. "In that case we'd better wait up for the others so they don't stray off."

"Yeah. C'mon. Let's have a quick look."

They arrived at a point where they could see

193

clear sky through the tree line. "We're on a ridge," Calvin said.

"Right," Blue said. "Let's have a look down this way to see if there is an easy way out of here."

They went another twenty meters. Suddenly the ground gave way under them as the rotted vegetation on which they'd been walking caved in under their weight. Both Black Eagles tumbled through a heavy line of brush, then rolled uncontrolled down a steep hill. Blue and Calvin held onto their weapons with desperate grips during the bouncing fall. The radio over Calvin's shoulder kept hitting him in the head each time he spun down the hillside. Finally they hit the bottom. Still surprised and woozy, they sat up.

The startled Chinese soldiers, sitting around the cookfires in their bivouac, stared at the two Americans.

For an instant there was no move on either side. Then the Black Eagles reacted and began scrambling back up the same hill they'd just fallen from.

They were half way up before a dumbfounded Chinese non-commissioned officer finally came to life. *"Chi po!"*

Blue and Calvin were almost at the top when the first shots slapped the ground and brush around them. They broke into the cover of the woods, but didn't slow down. Calvin pulled the radio off his shoulder, speaking as he ran. "Falcon—this—This is—P-Point—Over!" When

194

Falconi answered the call, Calvin was forced to be word economical. "Chinese—chasing—us—over!"

"Okay," Falconi's calm reassuring voice came back. "Return directly to the column. Don't sweat the Chinese. Just come to papa."

Calvin looked back and saw the first of the fleeter footed Chinese soldiers appearing. "Haul balls, Blue!" he yelled.

More shots exploded in the rear. The fired bullets cracked around them as the pair picked up speed out of desperation.

"Gawd damn!" Blue yelled.

"Shee-yut!" Calvin said echoing the feeling.

Their boots pounded the forest floor as the adrenaline kicked in. Calvin glanced back over his shoulder and saw what appeared to him at the time to be the entire Red Chinese Army chasing them.

The incoming fire increased as did the high-pitched yelling of the pursuers:

"Chi po!"

"Kui hei nei sheung shau!"

"Hang-faan lai!"

A few full-automatic fusillades broke out from the Chinese. Some of them had finally realized they had a better chance of hitting their quarry by throwing out more bullets since careful aiming was out of the question.

Finally Blue and Calvin sighted the other Black Eagles. Falconi and the guys were off to the right, positioned just a couple of meters into the thicker brush.

195

"Keep going!" Falconi yelled at them.

"Aye, aye, sir!" Blue responded in naval fashion.

"Yes, sir!" Calvin yelled.

Falconi watched them disappear on into the woods. He cautioned the rest of the detachment. "Get ready! They'll be here in a few seconds."

The first of the Chinese soldiers burst into view. The expressions on their faces were combinations of rage, excitement, and determination. They were almost all firing all full automatic now, making a thundering roar among the trees.

Falconi wasn't impressed. "Fire! Fire! Fire!"

The Black Eagles volley was an enfilading type that hit the pursuers from the side. The muzzle velocities of the M16s swept the running troops off their feet, tumbling to the ground in heaps of protesting, screaming death and wounds.

The second wave arrived and suddenly stumbled to a halt at the sight of their brother soldiers sprawled out on the ground. It was a fatal hesitation. The swarm of 5.56 millimeter bullets whacked into them, completing the slaughter by dumping more bloody cadavers to the earth of their mother country.

The Black Eagles ceased fire long enough to replace their empty magazines will full ones. They had no sooner locked and loaded, then fresh Chinese shooting broke out to their rear. The bullets smacked into the trees, making evil slapping sounds.

"Enemy to the rear!" Top yelled.

The well-trained detachment whirled and delivered return fire. This slowed the Chinese from that direction, but there were too many of them to hold for long. Falconi's military mind raced to a sound tactical idea.

"Top! Archie! Malpractice!" he ordered loudly. "Move forward and engage, then break off and pull back."

The trio leaped up and charged. They sprayed bullets ahead of them as they advanced. The Chinese, caught unaware, gave up two dead before they fully recovered and delivered sustained return fire.

"Let's get!" Top bellowed.

The three Black Eagles immediately broke contact and rushed back toward the original location. Like Calvin and Blue earlier, they caught up with the detachment. But, instead of continuing their flight, they fell in on the rear of the unit position.

The Chinese, enraged and eager to wipe out the unknown enemy in their territory, rushed through the woods in ragged skirmish lines. Unable to spot their enemy, the commander urged his troops to even greater speed. Unknowingly, they ran straight into the Black Eagles field of fire.

Nine M16 rifles fired until the magazines were emptied. Then they were reloaded and again emptied into the frenzied group of Chinese who were swept down in whole groups.

Sudden silence fell over the scene.

"Everybody up," Falconi ordered.

Grimacing at the bloody cadavers, the Black

Eagles got to their feet and waited for their next orders. But before Falconi could say anything, new voices were heard not too far away.

"*Heung ni shue lai!*"

"*Fong ha!*"

"I suggest we get the hell out of here," Falconi said.

Archie was more than ready. "Which direction, sir?"

"The same one we came from," Falconi said. "We won't make much distance today, but maybe we can get away from those bastards."

"Christ!" Top complained. "There must be thousands of 'em!"

"This is the most populous nation on the face of the earth," Swift Elk reminded him.

The detachment formed into a column and followed after Archie. They retraced the steps they'd already taken, making everyone feel as if they weren't accomplishing a damned thing.

NVA General Truong Van stuck close to Paulo. Unarmed among two sets of enemies—Chinese and American—the North Vietnamese began to experience deep feelings of paranoia. He glanced at Paulo Garcia's M16 slung loosely over the Marine's shoulder. Truong positioned himself close to that weapon. If things turned bad, he planned to quickly wrestle it free and take out Falconi. Then he knew that somebody's bullets, American or Chinese, would bring his mission and life to an end. But if Falconi was dead, he wouldn't mind so much.

Truong didn't want to take out the Black Eagle commander unless it was absolutely necessary. There was still a chance that they would run into his co-conspirators Colonel Huong and Lieutenant Anh who could bring about Falconi's capture alive and kicking. That's what he really wanted.

Falconi allowed the detachment a fast twenty minutes of travel before he slowed things down once again. It was time to become more security conscious. He ordered Gunnar Olson and Malpractice McCorckel out as flankers. The Black Eagle commander was not all that sure that a complete break with the Chinese pursuers had been made. Even if it had, there was always the chance that other units would be called into the area as quickly as possible.

And he was right.

Gunnar Olson spotted green uniforms off to his left. There was no necessity in checking that out. He pulled back to the main column as quickly as he could. "Sir, we got comp'ny out to the left."

"Okay," Falconi said calmly. "Go out and fetch Malpractice back." He got on the Prick-Six and raised Archie on the radio with orders to return.

The Black Eagles spread out and positioned themselves behind whatever cover they could find. There would be no time to dig proper fighting holes or to improve on what nature had accidentally provided them. They used the trees, thick bushes, and even rises in the ground as things to put between themselves and the expected enemy attackers.

The first Chinese to appear was a hapless, unlucky point man. Obviously inexperienced and excited, he moved with the carelessness of a man not looking *out* for the enemy, but simply looking *for* them. He blindly walked between Ray Swift Elk and Top Gordon, before he almost literally bumped into Paulo Garcia. The Marine, who had been watching the soldier approach, waited until he was sure the man had spotted him. Paulo's single shot split the man's skull, making his cap appear to leap from his head.

The battle was on.

The Chinese farther back came sweeping forward in a stupid maneuver. They had no idea of the actual location of their enemy, but they attacked as if they did.

When the Black Eagles opened fire, they mowed down the first rank in only one roaring second. The second got a bit farther but suffered the same fate.

"Jesus!" Ray Swift Elk said to himself. "Fish in a barrel! Fish in a barrel!"

The third Chinese battle line went farthest. They leaped over the first two, pressing forward but finally collapsing under the steel-jacketed hail of Black Eagle bullets.

The fourth group only managed to get between the second and third before they, too, were slaughtered. When the firing ended, the area of woods in front of Falconi's detachment was a solid carpet of dead Chinese soldiers.

But the lieutenant colonel had no time to celebrate the victory. "On your feet!" he exclaimed in a hurry to get the hell out of the area. "Archie, let's head due east for awhile. We know there're more Chinese to the south. If we go west we'll end up back in North Vietnam."

Archie wordlessly stepped out as the men formed up behind him to follow. Falconi kept them moving at a steady pace for more than an hour. Finally, realizing they suffered from nervous as well as physical fatigue, the commanding officer ordered a halt.

A loose perimeter was formed up and the men went on fifty percent alert with half on guard while the other half napped and rested. The scene had become almost peaceful when newer menacing sounds were suddenly heard:

Enemy helicopters.

Swift Elk summed up everybody's feelings. "Shit!"

Falconi slowly shook his head. "Things are going from bad to worse. That response means there is a military chopper base close by."

Top nodded. "Stealing a helicopter would be better than stealing a fishing boat, sir."

"Yeah," Falconi agreed. "But we don't have a helicopter pilot among us."

"I can fly a helicopter, sir," Gunnar Olson said.

There was a moment of stunned silence.

Gunnar continued. "When I was in the gunship squadron with my cousin Erick Stensland, he gave me lessons. I used to fly quite a bit as a matter of fact. Before you guys came along I was going to apply for formal training back at the Fort Rucker school, but I got hooked on being a Black Eagle."

Falconi stared at the Minnesotan. "I think," he said calmly, "that we should find that airbase."

Chapter 19

Warrant Officer Kai Fong left the briefing room of the Tungsing Army Air Base and strode rapidly across the criss-crossed runways toward his Soviet-built Mi-4 Hound troop-carrying helicopter.

The big aircraft, its engine already warming up, sat on the pad waiting for him. As he approached the chopper, Kai noticed his crew chief sitting inside staring out the open door. Generally the energetic young airman would be impatiently gesturing to him to hurry—particularly with the type of mission they were about to fly.

Unidentified infiltrators had moved into the district and engaged Chinese ground troops in combat. In an effort to surround and contain the attackers, various helicopters were being sent off to nearby infantry units to ferry troops into the battle zone. Kai had received orders to participate in the operation a scant half hour earlier. His crew chief had preceded him to the flight line while he received more detailed instructions.

Kai stepped up the pace and trotted toward the Mi-4. He shouted loud to be heard over the engine noise. *"Wai!* Is everything prepared for departure?"

The crew chief simply stared at him.

Mildly irritated, Kai leaped aboard.

Archie Dobbs and Blue Richards pointed their M16s at him and gestured for the pilot to sit beside the crew chief on the canvas bench along the side of the fuselage. Archie leaned out the chopper and signaled toward the wooded area at the edge of the airbase.

Falconi with the six other detachment members, left the trees and raced across the open area to the helicopter. Paulo Garcia tightly held on to General Truong Van's arm as the group ran toward the escape aircraft. They piled inside. The lieutenant colonel and Gunnar Olson hurried forward to the cockpit.

Gunnar cranked the throttle on the collective and pulled up on it. The engine sped up and the helicopter eased upward. It gradually picked up speed as it ascended. Not wanting to hang around, the Black Eagle's impromptu pilot pushed forward a bit on the cyclic making the aircraft move straight ahead as it climbed. Then he glanced at the instrument panel. "What the hell?"

The instruments were all labeled in Russian and Chinese. Gunnar could guess what they meant, but he had to be sure. Falconi slipped the intercom earphones on both himself and the Norwegian-American.

"Can you read me, Gunnar?"

"Yes, sir," Gunnar answered. "We got problems. I'm not real sure what all the instruments are."

"Don't worry," Falconi assured him. "I read Russian." He began pointing them out. "Altimeter, air speed indicator, gyro compass—"

"That's enough, sir," Gunnar said. "With them I'll get us to the coast."

"Fine," Falconi replied. "We'll search out a fishing village with some docked boats and land there. A quick descent and rush to the vessel shouldn't be too much trouble."

"Relying on the shock of surprise, sir?"

"Damned right."

Gunnar turned the helicopter directly onto a course of one-eighty and tipped the nose more to pick up speed. The Chinese countryside was amazingly beautiful. Rice paddies and villages were spread out in checkerboard arrangements with narrow dirt roads connecting them all. Everything seemed placid at the moment. The entire detachment, with General Truong Van and two Chinese prisoners in tow, was flying safely toward freedom.

Then the voice popped up over the earphones: *"Fei-kei mat-ma? Fei-kei mat-ma?"*

"What the hell is that?" Gunnar asked.

"Damn!" Falconi swore. He had a rough working knowledge of Cantonese picked up at a Special Forces officer orientation course for Red China. "They're asking for an authentication code of some kind."

"What happens if we don't answer?" Gunnar wanted to know.

"This is a totalitarian state," Falconi explained. "They don't allow aircraft, even when assigned missions, to suddenly take off without having the pilot prove who he is."

"Tell them something, sir," Gunnar urged his commanding officer. "Even if it's too let 'em know you don't understand."

"Good idea," Falconi said. He pulled the microphone off the instrument panel and pushed the transmit button. *"Ts'ing nei tsoi kong,"* Falconi said. He repeated it three times. "I told him to repeat himself."

The Chinese radio operator did, but this time Falconi simply ignored him. Gunnar grinned. "I think I'll put on some more speed."

"That's a damned good idea."

Gunnar maintained a straight course for a bit more than a quarter of an hour. He suddenly reached over and tugged on Falconi's sleeve. He pulled back on the cyclic bringing the helicopter to a hover as he pressed the left rudder pedal to swing the chopper over to face in that direction. "Look, sir! Just what the doctor ordered!"

Falconi looked through the lower viewing glass. A small village on the coast was nestled in a cozy cove. Several fishing vessels, all appearing to be motorized, were moored on a small dock. "Can you set this baby down next to those boats?"

"Can a whore make a soldier smile?" Gunnar said answering the question with the old stock military reply. He changed the helicopter's attitude, making a diving run toward the village.

They swept lower until a chilling sight suddenly appeared to their direct front.

Three Chinese gunships had come into view and made a non-firing strafing run at them. Another Chinese voice came over the air. *"Fei-kei ch'eung!"*

"He wants us to return to the airfield," Falconi said.

"Fuck him," Gunnar said. "As a matter of fact, fuck him very much!"

The Chinese hovered in front of them, showing every intention of forcing Gunnar to turn inland. Falconi thought fast. "Fake a return, then head west as fast as this bird will fly. We'll see what we can do in North Vietnamese territory."

"That's a ways off, sir," Gunnar warned him.

"We have no other choice," Falconi said grimly. "Fly, Gunnar! Fly!"

"Comrade Lieutenant!" the communications sergeant shouted.

Lieutenant Anh, idling against the rail on the flying bridge, looked up. "Yes, Comrade Sergeant?"

"The signals are growing stronger," the sergeant said listening over the earphones. "And very rapidly too!"

Colonel Huong now appeared on the bridge. He, too, was excited. "The boat's radio operator reports much Chinese radio traffic. They are involved in some sort of frantic action which is drawing closer."

"The comrade general's tracking signals are fast drawing closer," Anh reported. "Even now he is approaching this location."

The sergeant interrupted. "They are stronger in the air. See how they increase when I point the radio tracking receiver upward?"

Huong frowned in puzzlement. "What could be causing such a strange thing?"

Anh quickly figured it out. "He is in an aircraft, Comrade Colonel."

"Of course! But what could his situation be?" Huong asked. "Has he stolen such an aircraft? Or perhaps the Black Eagles have acquired one."

"Yes," Anh agreed. "It might even ben an American helicopter. There may have been some contingency plan we were unable to learn about."

"I will order our own aircraft to get airborne," Huong said.

"What are we to do?" Anh asked.

"If the escape helicopter cannot be retrieved safely, then we must shoot it down," Huong said. "Even with Comrade General Truong Van inside."

"Yes," Anh agreed. "Those are our orders."

"The loss of our respected superior officer will be greatly offset by the realization of the deaths of the Black Eagles," Huong reminded him.

"What's that down there?" Gunnar asked, pointing through the cockpit glass in the lower portion of the helicopter nose.

Falconi peered through the viewing area. "Some sort of torpedo boats," he answered. "They're sporting the Red Chinese flag."

"Then I suppose it wouldn't be advisable to seek their help," Gunnar said.

"That's right," Falconi answered with a grin. "Keep flying!"

"Uff da!" Gunnar said.

The Mi-4 continued its flight through the sky. The other helicopters kept up the pursuit. They came in close but made no overt hostile moves.

"I'm surprised they haven't started blasting us," Gunnar said.

"They don't know what's going on for sure," Falconi said. "The senior officer is probably going nuts trying to figure out if we've simply got radio trouble or not. Remember this bird wasn't reported as stolen. The pilot and crew chief are still aboard. As far as the Chinese know, they're operating this thing."

"Yeah? Wait'll those guys get close enough to see a blond, blue-eyed Norwegian in the driver's seat," Gunnar said.

"Let's hope they don't," Falconi said. He looked up in the wide-angled rear view mirror. "Hey! They're dropping back. No! They're turning back!"

"Hey, great!" Gunnar said. "I'll bet those guys were put on our tails right after coming back from a mission. They're prob'ly low on fuel."

Falconi tapped their own gas gauge. "Well, we're in damned good shape in that department."

"Good, sir. I think we're gonna have to do a hell of a lot more flying," Gunnar said. "There's three more boats down there."

"Yeah," Falconi replied spotting them. "Different flags too. I'd say they were North Vietnamese."

"Christ!" Gunnar complained. "Aren't there any friendlies at all around here?"

"Doesn't appear so," Falconi said. "Whoops!" he added. "One of those boats has a helicopter landing pad on it."

"Is the chopper there?" Gunnar asked.

"I don't see it," Falconi replied.

"That, sir, is definitely not a good sign," Gunnar said.

Further conversation was interrupted by Lieutenant Ray Swift Elk's sudden appearance in the cockpit. He grabbed the spare intercom set off the bulkhead and spoke into it. "Hey! I thought you'd be interested in knowing there's a North Vietnamese helicopter gunship closing in on us. And it looks very, very hostile."

Colonel Huong leaned closer to the loudspeaker that the patrol boat's radio operator had turned on for use in lieu of earphones. He nudged the sailor with an impatient shove. "Ask the comrade pilot what is happening up there?"

"*Tau* to *May Truc-Thang*, please advise us with a situation report."

The pilot's voice crackled over the speaker. "I

see a Red Chinese helicopter. Close observation shows three Oriental men and a number of white men on board. Orders?"

Anh gripped Colonel Huong's shoulder. "Please, Comrade Colonel. Give the situation careful consideration."

Huong turned around. "We have our orders, Comrade Lieutenant."

"Yes, Yes. Of course," Anh said. He had received the instructions to sacrifice General Truong Van if necessary in a cold-blooded manner. The young lieutenant had even mulled them over in his mind in a calm detached manner as any military man would. But now, in the stark reality of the situation, some of his self-confidence had eroded. "But we must contact the Chinese aircraft, *kong co?*"

Huong, an old campaigner who had buried many a comrade, hesitated a moment. But he relented. "Very well." He looked at the operator. "Contact the Red Chinese aircraft."

The sailor shrugged. "*Toi tec*, Comrade Colonel. I do not know their frequency."

"Try any frequency!" Anh shouted. "They must be contacted immediately!"

"But, Comrade Lieutenant! There are many," the radioman said. "I cannot possibly find the right one in a short amount of time."

Huong's face was stern as he faced the young lieutenant. "You are a soldier of world socialism, Comrade Lieutenant."

"Yes, Comrade Colonel," Anh replied softly.

211

"You have duties to perform," Huong reminded him. "Some may be unpleasant and even involve the death of your closest friends. But you must perform those duties without hesitation."

Anh nodded his head.

"I order you to do your duty," Huong said.

"Yes, Comrade Colonel." Anh turned to the radio operator. "Contact the helicopter gunship and instruct him to shoot down the Chinese aircraft."

"*Co*, Comrade Lieutenant!" the sailor said. He spoke into the microphone. "*Tau* to *May Bay Truc-Thang*. Destroy the Chinese helicopter!"

"Repeat the message," Huong ordered.

"Destroy the Chinese helicopter!"

Gunnar took another reassuring look at the fuel gauge, happy to again see the guarantee there was plenty of fuel left. He decided to make a slight westerly swing to begin an approach to the coast.

But suddenly the helicopter shook and rattled.

Gunnar glanced up in time to see the North Vietnamese gunship roar past and make a turn toward his rear. "He's making his moves."

"I'd say so," Falconi said. "How're the controls?"

"Still A-Okay," Gunnar reported. He looked at the instrument panel. "You don't see anything on there that indicates a weapons system, do you?"

"I'm afraid not," Falconi said. "But we've got some guys with M16s in the back. I'm going back there and get on the crew chief's intercom. Listen for my instructions."

"You know I got to bring this bird to a standstill hover before I can swing that tail around, don't you?" Gunnar said. "If I try any fast turns while moving forward, this thing is going to bank and some of the guys are going to be pitched out into the sky."

"Nobody said this job was going to be easy," Falconi said. "I'll tell you what to do."

"Yes, sir," Gunnar said. "I've got that rearview mirror. I'll try to make some decisions too."

"Good luck," Falconi said going back to the troop compartment.

Gunnar headed for the coast, but kept an eye on that mirror and his ears tuned in on the intercom. Falconi's voice came in loud and clear. "Swing, Gunnar!"

Gunnar hauled back on the cyclic and kicked in the right rudder. He could barely hear the guys' M16 rifles blasting at the North Vietnamese helicopter.

"Straighten up and go!"

Gunnar swung back to face the west and resumed the run for safety. Back in the troop compartment, the Black Eagles prepared for the next strafing run by the enemy chopper. Falconi watched as best he could by leaning out the opening while strapped into the crew chief's seat. But this time it was Gunnar who first saw the coming attack.

The chopper pulled up and whipped around so

fast the men were pitched against each other. They brought up the M16s and waited for the NVA chopper to appear. When it did, they cut loose. Expended cartridges bounced off the deck and bulkheads as the full-automatic volley belched like fire out toward the aircraft streaking past the troop door.

The two Chinese crewmen, confused as hell to begin with, could not fathom what was going on. They were prisoners in their own helicopters, held there by a bunch of wild-eyed Americans. There was also a North Vietnamese officer along, but he seemed passive as if the Yankees were among his best friends. Finally, the Chinese pilot came to the conclusion that North Vietnam had evidently gotten on the side of the U.S.A. for an invasion of Red China.

His mind raced, *"Kong maan ti*—I don't understand!"

Truong Van, on the other hand, understood all too well. From the actions of the gunship, he knew that Colonel Huong had ordered the Chinese helicopter he was riding in shot down. His face paled and he clenched his fist. He had reached the end of his life.

The pilot in the North Vietnamese chopper had grown wary of zipping past the open troop door on the right side of the target aircraft. A couple of shots had splattered against his own helicopter, and he knew that with that many rifles firing at him, he also stood a chance of being blasted out of the sky. He carefully lined up for his next strafing run, then tipped forward and roared in, the machine guns in his nose blazing away.

He waited for the Chinese aircraft to come into a hover and spin. But this time he pulled off to the left. Now he skidded sideways and raked the other helicopter with a devastating spray of heavy slugs.

Gunnar slammed the cyclic over, but it wouldn't respond to his efforts. Next he tried the collective. The throttle worked, but it bounced up and down with all the normal tension gone. A little experimentation told him he could go forward or backward, but any fancy maneuvers were out of the question.

"Sir!" he shouted into the microphone of the intercom. "We've had it."

"What's the matter, Gunnar?" came back Lieutenant Colonel Robert Falconi's voice.

"I'm losing the aircraft, sir. A couple of more hits and we'll take an uncontrolled dive into the sea!" Gunnar advised him.

"Okay, Gunnar," Falconi said in an amazingly calm voice. "Take us in low over the water. Then slow her down to almost a hover. We'll all jump out into the ocean and make a swim for shore."

"Shore?" Gunnar asked. "Christ, sir! The last time I looked it was fifteen kilometers away!"

"That's the distance I estimated too," Falconi said.

"I'd like to remind you we've got no flotation gear aboard," Gunnar said. "No inflatable rafts, no life jackets, no nothing."

215

"And I'd like to remind you that we have no choice," Falconi said. "Take us down."

The helicopter shook again under hits from the North Vietnamese. Gunnar gritted his teeth and headed toward the drink.

Chapter 20

The helicopter's tail swung back and forth as the aircraft skimmed the waves. The men inside, with the exception of the two frightened and thoroughly confused Chinese, stripped down to their underwear. Truong Van, knowing he was going into the water, sacrificed the radio tracking transmitter as he peeled out of his own clothing. His grandiose plans were now forgotten. The only thing he had on his mind was to concentrate on the long swim back to the North Vietnamese coast and whatever safety was available to him there.

The chopper lurched heavily as another fusillade of machine gun fire slammed into it. The Chinese crew chief slumped forward, his torso turned into torn meat. The pilot Kai Fong grabbed his friend, smearing himself with blood as he held on to him. He was in total shock now. Falconi leaned over and shouted in his ear that his friend was dead and that they had a long swim to make. But Kai Fong was incapable of responding. None of the Black Eagles had the time to give the Chinese warrant officer any help.

Gunnar continued to battle the shuddering helicopter. He tried to throttle back to reduce the air pressure on the aircraft's shattered hull, but now that instrument would not respond to his touch. Suddenly the cockpit glass shattered on his side of the chopper. Gunnar checked their altitude and saw they were skimming the waves. There was nothing to do but lock down the controls and get out.

He slipped out of the seat and through the hatch to the troop compartment. He could see the other guys poised to leap out. "Unass this bird!" Gunnar yelled. "I'll undress in the water."

Falconi turned to the man nearest the door. It was Blue Richards. Leaping from helicopters was old stuff to the Navy Seal. He got the signal from Falconi and went through the door. The others, including General Truong Van, piled out after him. Only the two Chinese—one alive and one dead—remained aboard the Mi-4.

The Black Eagles quickly bobbed to the surface. They were just in time to watch the North Vietnamese helicopter deliver the *coup de grace*. Heavy machine gun fire poured into the Chinese aircraft until it abruptly exploded into bright orange flame and hit the water. It sank immediately, leaving an oily black plume of smoke drifting across the waters of the Gulf of Tonkin.

But the Black Eagles' problems were far from over.

The gunship swung around then swept down toward them, its machine guns once again blazing hot slugs. The first bullets hit a few meters in front of the detachment, throwing up nasty spurts of salt water. The men barely had time to dive and swim deep before the volley reached them.

They dove as deep as they could, hearing the drawn out "zip" of bullets slowed abruptly by the water.

Finally, in need of air, they surfaced. Falconi took a deep breath. He could see the North Vietnamese helicopter positioning itself for another strafing run. The men, still out of breath, sucked in air and prepared to go underwater once again in what could eventually lead to complete exhaustion.

Falconi knew the end of the Black Eagles had arrived.

Chapter 21

Lieutenant Colonel Falconi, the salt water burning his eyes, looked around at each of his men. He could see their heads appearing among the waves:

Ray Swift Elk, Top Gordon, Buffalo Soldier Culpepper, Malpractice McCorckel, Gunnar Olson, Blue Richards, Archie Dobbs, and Paulo Garcia still sticking close to General Truong Van.

The Black Eagle commander knew this was the last he would ever see of them. He'd always hoped that if the unit was wiped out, it would be in the glory of a fighting battle making a Foreign Legion style last stand. As a combat commander, if he was to go down in defeat he wanted to do it while knee-deep in enemy dead.

But, as much as he regretted and hated it, they faced an ignoble death. They would die being helplessly strafed in the open ocean while bobbing around like apples in a tub of water.

Hardly the kind of death professional soldiers would hope for.

Now, after numerous dives to avoid the strafing runs, everyone was exhausted. The men's labored breathing could be heard as they treaded water. Swimming was out of the question. The North Vietnamese helicopter gunship had made a wide lazy turn as if the pilot knew this would be the last and final run. Falconi, his heart filled with hatred but not fear, watched almost detached as the chopper began boring in. He raised his fist and extended the middle finger.

Archie Dobbs' voice sounded an epitaph over the sound of the approaching engine. "You guys are the greatest!"

The chopper was perfectly lined up for the killing flight. With its nose tipped slightly forward in the proper firing attitude, it came boring in. The aircraft looked like a giant shark out of water closing in on its prey.

Suddenly the sea seemed to boil in front of the Black Eagles. Foam and violent splashing so disturbed the waves that Falconi at first thought an underwater earthquake had occurred.

Then the conning tower of the *Perch* rose out of the water. Its unexpected appearance between them and the attacking chopper provided the cover that they needed. For a brief moment the men stared in uncomprehending shock at the submarine. Top, as usual, snapped them out of any lethargy.

"You dumb shits like treading water? Head for that goddamn sub! Move it! *Move it!*"

Cheering, the Black Eagles swam toward the *Perch* as this new occurrence renewed their flagging physical strength. Now Archie changed his shouting. "*Calcitra clunis,* guys!"

Sailors appeared from the hatches dragging a .50 caliber Browning anti-aircraft machine gun with them. It took the well-drilled submariners only seconds to set it up. The weapon was already

221

chattering when the North Vietnamese gunship appeared overhead. The helicopter went up in a lazy arc with flames coming out the rear. Then it nosed over and crashed into the ocean.

Chuck Fagin's head now could be seen looking down at them. He was grinning. "Hey! If you guys are through swimming we can leave now."

Once again Falconi extended that middle finger.

The three-boat Chinese squadron, its torpedo tubes primed and ready, skimmed over the waves toward the trio of North Vietnamese patrol vessels.

Captain Mung was damned good and angry. He had seen the gunship shoot down the Chinese helicopter. Such an outrageous act of war could not be unanswered. Neither he nor his exec Lieutenant Chiang knew what their aircraft was doing out so far on the Gulf of Tonkin nor did they care. They had personally seen it strafed from the sky.

On board the command boat of the North Vietnamese Squadron, Colonel Huong and Lieutenant Anh watched in horror as the Chinese flotilla bore in on them. The torpedoes were launched and hit the water, bouncing up once, before settling down for their well-aimed run.

Stunned and frightened, the two North Vietnamese officers watched the wakes of the explosive devices draw closer to their patrol boats.

It was the last thing they were ever to see.

Epilogue

"I don't know if Truong Van is a genuine defector or not," Lieutenant Colonel Falconi admitted.

"He's an enigmatic guy," Fagin said. "And don't let anybody fool you. He is one tough sonofabitch."

"No matter. He's singing his heart out to SOG's G2 like it was a command performance," Falconi said. "When he came aboard the *Perch*, the general was in his underwear like the rest of us. If he carried any secret documents, they're in the Gulf of Tonkin with his uniform." He sat across from the CIA officer at the dining table in Andrea Thuy's apartment. The Black Eagle commander took another bite of the baked ham. "The guy has no choice now. If his defection was a phony set up to grab us, it went down the tubes. That means his superiors will be highly embarrassed one way or the other."

"Right," Fagin agreed. "The North Vietnamese general staff are going to list him as a defector just to save their asses from KGB justice."

Andrea, who had gone to the kitchen to fetch some more rolls, joined them. "My own opinion is that he was a renegade who tried to pull this off on his own and it went kaput. We've gotten a lot of reports out of the north that the NVA is growing pretty disenchanted with the Russian's heavy handedness. At any rate, the truth behind the matter doesn't mean a thing now. Truong is ours for good." She passed the rolls around. "How are the guys doing?"

"Great," Falconi said. "Taggart is letting them spend a few days in Saigon before we return to Nui Dep."

"You may not get back there," Fagin said.

There was dead silence around the table.

Falconi finally spoke. "What are you getting at?"

"Nothing."

Andrea glared at him. "Don't lie to us, Chuck Fagin. You've gotten word on another Black Eagle operation, haven't you?"

"I'm not saying I have and I'm not saying I haven't," Fagin said smugly. "Pass the ham, please."

Falconi gave him the platter.

Fagin helped himself to a large slab. "By the way," he said almost absent-mindedly. "How are you at knocking out Soviet tanks?"

"Oh, Christ!" Falconi moaned. "Tanks!"

"Like you always said, old friend," Fagin said smugly. "Nobody told you this job would be easy."